SUBMERGED CITY

DROWNED EARTH

DROWNED EARTH

Eight novellas.
Eight Australian authors.
One watery apocalypse.

Scientists said that it would take 5000 years for Earth's oceans to rise.

They were wrong.

After an asteroid collides with Antarctica, a tsunami devastates the world's coastal cities and escalates the melting of the ice caps.

These eight novellas set in various locations around Australia explore the potential consequences of such a catastrophe. They can be read in any order.

Prequel short story: Shards of Silver by Alanah Andrews
The Rise by Sue-Ellen Pashley
Fire Over Troubled Water by Nick Marone
Submerged City by Austin P. Sheehan
Tides of War by Marcus Turner
The Jindabyne Secret by Jo Hart
River of Diamonds by S. M. Isaac
Salvaged by C.A. Clark
Emoto's Promise by Shel Calopa

SUBMERGED CITY

AUSTIN P. SHEEHAN

DROWNED EARTH

DEDICATION

This is dedicated to my wife who has supported and believed in me long before I even believed in myself.

Submerged City is also dedicated to all victims of abuse and sexual assault, to those who said #metoo and to those who were too scared, too ashamed or just not safe enough to do so.

Please be aware that there are two scenes of sexual assault in the novella.

And if you are a victim of sexual assault or domestic violence and need assistance or support, call 1800RESPECT for Australia's national sexual assault and domestic violence counselling service.

CHAPTER ONE

A deep, terrible growl—the grinding and shaking of ancient bones—rattled David into consciousness. He lay on the salvaged mattress he used for a bed, now wide awake, waiting for the next tremor—for the sudden falling sensation telling him it was already too late.

"It's the Rydges hotel," whispered Salim, squatting by the window, binoculars in hand. "Come see."

David rubbed his tired eyes and his rough, stubble-coated cheeks, and found his way to Salim in the darkness.

The full moon shone on the city, illuminating the foaming crests of the waves as they crashed against the buildings, dark shapes like tombstones against a backdrop of stars. Through the binoculars, David looked down Exhibition Street to the hotel. It trembled and a hideous groan echoed through the city. The building couldn't have much time left. As David watched, the E from the RYDGES sign fell, crashing into the angry sea. He prayed everyone had already escaped—but perhaps prayer wasn't the right word. Any faith he may once have had was washed away with Linda, with everyone else in the city.

The hotel shuddered and collapsed into itself, sinking into the sea, metre by metre. Figures jumped from the upper windows into the churning waters as the building fell apart. *Shit.* David put his hand on Salim's shoulder as the building split into chunks of concrete and glass, falling into the foaming waves.

Salim jerked to his feet. "We've got to help them, Da!"

"They're too far away. It's too late."

"No, we've got to try," insisted Salim.

"I'm sorry—"

"I'll go without you!" He slipped out of David's grasp and headed for the stairs.

With a sigh, David weighed his options. Sal was an orphan of the waves, and David had no real authority over the teenager. But he always tried to look out for him, tried to be a good father figure.

"Okay," he called as Sal reached the top of the stairwell. "Prep the boat. I'll grab the torches."

Salim's smile lit the darkness before he disappeared down the stairs. David pulled on a jacket, grabbed a torch and some rope from the bench where they kept their salvage gear, before following Salim downwards.

Their small boat was docked inside the fifth floor of the office building, the broken windows leaving the entire floor open to the sea. Salim was in the boat already, his quick dark hands untying the knots. David waded through the water to the side of the boat, pulled himself in and reached for the oars. The old tinny had an engine, but petrol was scarce—only the Mainland Militia could afford to use it. David and Salim had learned to row well together over the months they'd known each other and they matched each other's strokes, sending the boat through the smashed windows that let the ocean inside.

"Sal, listen up," David said. "You know how dangerous the sea can be during the day, but it's even worse at night."

"I know, Da." Salim rolled his eyes in the moonlight.

"Okay, just stay sharp."

Gripping their oars, adrenaline and determination running through their veins, they fought against the waves twenty-odd metres above what used to be Exhibition Street, now the ocean floor. The remaining towers on either side stood like monoliths, bursting out of the sea. Where people had made their homes in the surviving buildings, candle-light flickered through the windows high above the dark water.

Screams and shouts for help sounded over the steady crash of the waves as they approached the devastation. Rubbish—milk bottles, plastic bags, driftwood—littered the turbulent water. At the pit of David's gut lay a nauseous, icy dread. Ahead of them, other boats had already converged on the sunken building and jagged beams of light scanned the rough sea, looking for survivors.

David's heart lurched, something moved under the water—a fish? A shark? No—a hand!

"Over there!" David pointed to where he saw the movement.

Salim pulled off his olive green hoodie and dived into the dark, churning water.

David held his breath. The waters amongst the ruins were full of hidden danger and were even more treacherous at night. He scanned the area where Salim had disappeared. Nothing. *How much time had passed? Ten seconds? Thirty?*

After an agonising minute, Salim finally broke the

surface, gasping for air. He lifted a pallid and lifeless head above the waves.

As David leant over to pull the figure into the boat, the sound of approaching speedboats echoed through the city.

"Shit, they're coming. We've gotta get out of here!" David grabbed the figure by the arms and pulled. The boat tilted, close to capsizing. Desperate, his muscles taut with strain, David kept pulling, dragging the sodden and limp figure over the edge.

Sal hauled himself into the boat and started rhythmically pressing down on the chest of the unconscious man.

"We've got to go!" David shouted over the roar of the speedboats.

Sal kept working on the pallid, pale man while David grabbed the oars and rowed, trying to get them out of sight, heart racing, full of adrenaline and fear.

"This way!" called an urgent voice from his left. Without thinking, he turned the boat towards the familiar voice. They needed to get out of the water before the militia arrived. Salim was pressing down on the man's chest, breathing air into his lungs.

"Almost there!" called the voice, and the figure of Baker appeared, leaning through a broken window above the waterline. David pulled the oars inside the boat and threw the rope to his friend.

"Get through that window, Sal."

As Sal stood, the moonlight fell on the figure at the bottom of the boat. Hassan, a fellow salvager. *Shit.*

Hassan coughed and spluttered. *He was alive!* David scrambled to his feet, grabbed Hassan, and dragged him towards the window. Baker's hand, big and beefy, reached out and grabbed the half-drowned man. David jumped through the window, following Sal to safety. Danger only lay out on the water, as the Militia didn't take anyone from inside buildings—or at least they hadn't, yet.

David looked up to see four panicked faces: Baker, with his messy red hair; Freya, her brow creased with worry; Hassan, pale and shaking; and Salim.

"We've gotta get upstairs," said Freya. "Now!"

Salim and David, with Hassan between them, followed Baker and his daughter through the flooded apartment and up two flights of stairs.

"What's happening out there?" asked Salim, when they entered the apartment Baker and Freya had made their home.

"They're crawling all over the rubble," Freya replied, her voice tense.

"Have they found anyone?" asked Baker.

Freya nodded and pointed through the blinds. A

lone figure dressed in a faded army uniform stood guard over a jet black speedboat, a machine gun in her arms. Her sandy blonde ponytail glinted in the moonlight, whipping from side to side.

David's heart sank—several figures were in the boat, some lying motionless, others crouched, handcuffed.

"Can't we do anything, Da?" Salim asked, looking over to the corner where Baker kept his crossbow.

David put his hand on Sal's shoulder and let the darkness, the hopelessness and the despair answer for him.

CHAPTER TWO

Emma Ramsey sat in the back of a speedboat from the Essendon Fields Barracks, her eyes watching the figures huddled together; handcuffed, soaking wet and shaking with fear. She told herself that it was for their own good—they were being returned to the mainland to be treated for injuries, and for their own safety.

"We should just drag 'em all out of the city," Private Patersall yelled over the engines. "By their hair, kicking and screaming, whatever it takes."

"It'd save us a lot of these bullshit oh-three-hundred rescue missions," Private Fulham replied, his voice bitter as the boat crashed through the waves.

"Or at least put in a rule where if the buildings

collapse after midnight they have to fend for themselves, right Corporal?" Patersall asked, watching the terrified faces of the huddled figures.

"I agree," said Corporal Nelson, adjusting the frames of his glasses. "But you know what Messinger says: *We go where we're needed.*"

Emma's stomach squirmed as the boat slowed and swerved around the rooftops emerging from the dark water. The remaining buildings in the CBD were unsafe, yet many people still chose to live there. She knew that the mainland, too, was dangerous—even the inland towns which had been spared by the waves were targeted by raiders and looters. She shot a nervous glance at the water surrounding the boat. Surely it was still safer to be on solid ground.

"Stop! No!" A shout came from their right, from another speedboat dodging around the buildings.

As Emma watched, a figure jumped over the side of the other boat, the moonlight catching the handcuffs around their wrists, before they disappeared beneath the waves.

"Corporal, someone jumped!" Emma shouted.

Corporal Nelson watched the other speedboat. It didn't slow down. A searchlight scanned the water behind them, before shutting off.

"We should go and help," urged Emma.

"If they aren't going to stop, we're not either."

Emma watched the water, looking for any sign of the desperate escapee, but it was hopeless. The sea had claimed yet another victim.

***

After they had transferred their prisoners to the security division, Emma headed up the hill to the women's barracks, her heart heavy. It was the same every time one of those towers came down, rounding up the survivors and bringing them to the mainland. The injured would get medical treatment and transferred to a field hospital, and those with outstanding warrants or perceived as a possible threat to the community were sent to the prisons or labour camps.

She stopped to look south, towards the remaining towers hidden by the darkness. *How many people are still out there? How long can they last?* She shivered against the chill winds and turned her attention back to the Essendon Fields Barracks. Before the waves, it had been a small airfield. The hangars and buildings that had survived the tsunami had been converted into officers' quarters, a gym, a mess hall and medical, internment and storage facilities, all lit up by generators.

"Private Ramsey!"

Emma turned to face Corporal Nelson, his lanky figure looming over her, his eyes looking her up and down. "Yes, Corporal?" *What does this arsehole want now?*

"Don't forget the zero-nine-thirty patrol tomorrow."

"No, Corporal Nelson." *How could I forget? We do the same patrol every damn day.*

"As you were."

Shaking her head, Emma entered the women's barracks, asking herself why she stuck it out with the Defence Force. Why she let herself be ordered around, mocked and leered at by power-hungry wankers like Nelson.

The answer, of course, was simple. After Jagannatha crashed into Antarctica, after the wave washed her whole life away, she'd wanted to help. Simply to help. And the city, the millions of people broken by the flood, needed all the help they could get. A small part of her had wanted to return to the small town where her parents still lived, but she couldn't abandon her adopted home, couldn't turn her back on so much need and heartache.

The state had been put under martial law soon after the tsunami, and what remained of the city's emergency services had been absorbed into the Defence Force. Hoping to reunite families and rebuild communities, Emma had signed up. When she heard General Messinger's catchphrase, 'we go where we're needed' her heart lifted. This was where she was needed, and she knew she had made the right decision. But now, six months after the disaster, there were still thousands and thousands of people without homes, broken families and orphaned children. There was still so much to do.

As the waves crashed against distant houses, Emma felt more than ever that the Defence Force's priorities had changed. Instead of cleaning up and rebuilding the city, rehoming the needy and vulnerable, they were policing the survivors. And she hadn't signed up to be a cop.

All the hard work—clearing the roads and highways, rebuilding the bridges, even collecting the corpses—was being done by the labour crews. These prisoners, under the supervision of the heavy-handed security division, were being bullied and threatened into doing the work no-one wanted to do. Except that Emma did want to do it. She'd rather collect corpses from flooded houses than create new ones through enforcing Messinger's law.

Every morning, the briefing was the same. Resources were scarce, some parts of the city had running water, other parts had electricity, few had both. And crime rates were increasing every day.

The futility of it weighed her down. After an event such as Jagannatha, people should be coming together, not tearing each other apart.

As Emma took off her faded uniform, the bushes rustled outside the window. She froze, feeling prying eyes explore her body. Her skin crawled and anger welled up inside her. It was the second time this week someone had spied on her, and she had a good idea who it was. Too tired to confront them, she turned off the lights and slipped under the covers. She'd already complained to Captain Rynard, the base's commanding officer, who couldn't care less. Still, she was safe inside the barracks. If she had been a civilian outside the barbed-wire-fence, though ... Emma's stomach churned with disgust. She knew how frequent sexual assaults were, and how seriously they were taken by the men in the Defence Force.

With a heavy heart she sat in the empty room, lost and alone. Private Josephine Avery used to fill the silence and know exactly what to say to lift Emma's mood, but she'd been reassigned to the Ferntree Gully base almost a month ago. Emma understood why her friend had been transferred—Jo was an ambulance driver, and she was needed in the eastern suburbs where the hospitals had survived the wave.

But that didn't make it any easier for Emma. The

only other women left at Essendon Fields were the doctors and nurses who worked at the temporary field hospital, and they were always too busy to talk. She couldn't talk to the men here, not if she wanted to be listened to. Not if she had to get something off her chest. It wasn't just that the Defence Force had done so little in terms of rebuilding the city, or the sexual harassment, or even the loneliness that was getting to Emma. She was running out of hope. As she closed her eyes, one of Messinger's first radio broadcasts came back to her.

"Do not lose hope, do not lose heart." Messinger's booming voice crackled over the PA system. "We have survived the wave. We have survived the darkness. God has seen fit to spare us, and in doing so has issued us a challenge. With his grace, we shall overcome adversity."

Emma sighed. How optimistic they had all been. People rallied behind Messinger, behind his message of hope. While many had lost their faith along with their loved ones, they still needed hope, and Messinger gave it to them. At first, anyway. And when the initial hope had run out, people wanted someone to blame.

Messinger gave them that, too.

"The floodgates have opened!" he had proclaimed, reminding Emma of the fire-and-brimstone priest in her childhood town. "And who opened them?

By God, we did. We opened the floodgates of damnation by allowing, no, encouraging sin and stupidity to flourish. You know what I'm talking about. God created men and women to populate the Earth, and now God needs men and women to repopulate it."

Emma rolled over, trying to block out the echoes from the past.

Over the months, it had become clear Messinger's conservative beliefs had been strengthened through the disaster. He saw the tsunami as the righteous wrath of his God, angered by the sins of humanity. It wouldn't have been so bad if it was only one man with these idiotic, hateful ideas, but Messinger was a powerful man with plenty of supporters—not just inside the ADF, but on the other side of the barbed-wire fence too. Emma was careful to watch what she said these days.

Still, Messinger wasn't the only person to have kept their faith. Stories had trickled through the barracks of Muslims and Jews opening their places of worship as emergency shelters, of Christians and Hindus working together to rebuild homes. *Doing our job.* She'd lost count of the number of times she'd convinced herself to leave the army, to find another way of helping survivors of the flood. Yet, every time, the fear for her own safety convinced her to stay.

CHAPTER THREE

"Charity Donescu. Sandeep Singh. Imogen Patterson. Stefan Boynton." His hand on Salim's shoulder, David listened as the names of the deceased, missing, and captured were read out. Each was a friend, each name hurt like a knife in the chest.

In the morning light, the sea-bound community had gathered on Central Island, a large makeshift raft anchored above the ruins of the State Library and Melbourne Central. They took stock of those who had been lost in the collapse of the hotel and those taken by the Defence Force. Hundreds of seagulls surrounded the gathering, perched on the ruins—and on the island itself—as if in solidarity with the community.

When the last name had been read, Alfred stepped forward, his thin grey hair blowing in the wind. "Let's bow our heads in silence, taking a minute to think of those we have lost." His voice was low and full of grief.

David closed his eyes, thinking of his friends lost in the collapse of the Rydges Hotel. Thinking of the six lost when the 140 William Street office sank last month. Thinking of the millions lost when the tsunami tore through the city, and those who had perished in the weeks of darkness and despair after the wave. And Linda. There was an emptiness inside him, an emptiness which could only be filled by one thing. *I need a drink.* He shuddered and opened his eyes, pushing the thought away. *No, I'm not that person anymore.*

The triangular head of the ME Bank building watched on in silence, itself dwarfed by the smooth curved glass of the Aurora skyscraper, still new when the wave had struck. To the east stood the grey and white towers above the drowned QV shopping centre, home to many of the survivors—and to many more ghosts.

"Elise. Alfred. Everyone." Corinne's grim eyes searched the group as she held her daughter close to her chest. "How long can we keep this up? We're losing more people all the time. It's not safe here. For us, for our children. For Ivy." She looked down at the child in her arms.

"You're right, Corinne," conceded Elise. "It isn't safe. But I've not heard of any place that is."

"The mainland—"

"Doesn't have buildings that collapse. But it's got its own dangers." Elise's voice was soft, but under her closely cropped hair, her face was lined with concern.

Hassan crossed his arms over his chest. "I agree with Elise. A lot of us came here to get away from Messinger's Militia; from the persecution, from the beatings, from the blame. I almost died last night, but I'm still not going back."

"Corinne, no-one's being kept here against their will." Baker's red hair swept back in the wind as he spoke. "If you want to return to the mainland or take a boat east or west to search for another home, you can. But we'll all be safer if we stick together."

"I know everyone's scared," said Kintha, looking at Corinne with warmth in her eyes. "But I love our community. We all look out for each other, we help each other, and we respect each other. And importantly, we're free to be ourselves." She smiled as she looked around the group, at her friends—her family. "On the mainland, everyone is fending for themselves, all under the steel-clad boots of the militia. We're lucky they only bother us when a building comes down."

A murmur of agreement rippled around the

crowd.

"These are dark times, testing times." Alfred's voice drifted away with the salty breeze. "We will mourn for those lost, but we need to stay strong."

"Can't we do anything for the people the Militia took?" asked Salim, looking helplessly around the group. Another dagger in David's heart.

"We can't, Sal. You know that." A sympathetic smile crossed Elise's weathered face. "I wish we could, but we don't have the manpower or the weapons to take on the army."

Salim's body shook with anger beneath his olive hoodie. David squeezed his shoulder—he was proud of the kid, of his strength and passion. *Linda would have loved him.*

"We can't stop the buildings collapsing, but we can make it easier for people to get out." Alfred looked up at the remaining towers, pillars of grey, blue, brown and white. "Most of the people we lost lived high up. They didn't have enough time to get out. So anyone who lives higher than six floors above the sea, you need to move to a lower floor."

"How about emergency exits?" asked Baker. "Like a rope ladder out of a window?"

"I like it." Elise flashed a smile. "People can climb out instead of jumping."

"You know, if we had enough rope, we could even create bridges between buildings," said Kintha.

"Not a bad idea." Alfred nodded, glancing up at the towers.

"Do we have enough rope?" David asked.

"I'm not sure," said Elise. "Let's all come back tonight, with as much rope as we can find."

***

David and Salim rowed above La Trobe Street, past the top two levels of what remained of the squat, concrete Federal Police office. Behind that, a tower rose into the sky; a mishmash of shapes and angles, tinted dark glass and white steel. The tattered clothing which hung over various balconies was the only sign it was still inhabited.

The water was shallow in this part of the city, and at low tide they had to be careful to avoid rubble and the wreckage of cars, trucks and trams beneath them. Salim often enjoyed seeing schools of fish or curious crabs exploring the cars, the sunken ships, and the broken furniture. But today he stared straight ahead, brow knotted, his olive-green hood pulled over his head.

"How are you feeling, Sal?"

"I'm pissed off. Nobody wants to help the people the militia took. Not even Elise, and she's always talking about doing the right thing."

"Don't get me wrong," said David, "Elise and Baker would love to fight back against Messinger's Militia. But when the name of the game is survival, you've gotta pick your battles."

"We've got guns."

"Not enough."

"We should've used them, stopped the militia taking the survivors, Da." Sal's voice shook with bitter anger. "We should have tried."

David looked at the ruined buildings emerging from the water. "Most of us came here to escape the violence of the mainland. The city's under Martial Law. What General Messinger says, goes. Right now, we are just an itch, just a tickle on his big fat belly. But if we turn our guns on his soldiers, he'd wipe us all out."

In silence, they rowed under heavy grey clouds, through waves and debris, to the cream-coloured Dockside Tower. The balconies of the few floors that emerged from the depths still protruded over what was once Spencer Street.

"There used to be a construction site near here," explained David. "Some billionaire spent millions on building a new tower here, but the wave came through when they'd just started. I figured it'd be a good place to look for ropes and chains." David put on his wetsuit, goggles and oxygen tank and lowered himself into the water. "I'll go first, scope out the scene."

David dove down, feeling the cool water and silence envelop him. It wasn't really silence, of course. There was noise underwater. Deep, eternal, constant noise. Constant danger too—but danger he knew. There were no monsters underwater, just fish, mammals and crustaceans. That was one reason he'd chosen to live with the city-dwelling community, all the monsters were on the land.

The Dockside Tower was a dark shadow to the right, and below him was chaos. No matter how many times he dived, he never got used to the scene. The bent and twisted shapes of train carriages, cars and sunken boats lay on the ocean floor amongst the ruins. *Linda always took the train.* For a moment the panic in her voice, her wild, terrified eyes came back to him.

David forced his attention back to the task at hand. There was constant movement under the surface—schools of small fish darted through car windows; plastic sheets, seaweed and football scarves bobbed and swayed with the water. But nothing big, nothing menacing. Not that he could see, anyway. He swam back to the surface to get Sal.

***

David sat in the boat while Salim dived below. The kid was a great diver—a natural. He had no fear, which concerned David, but the risks he took yielded reward. Many of their community's most valuable possessions were a result of Sal's dives. They were lucky to have him. And David was lucky to have found him—lost, terrified and alone—during the horrors of the weeks of darkness, when the dirt and dust from the asteroid's impact blotted out the sun. Being a friend, a father-figure to Sal kept David sane, gave him a purpose, and that all kept the bottle at bay.

The heavy clouds brought rain, and David took out an empty bucket from under the seat, never wasting an opportunity to get fresh water. To the north, a group of gulls were cawing, grouped on one of many small, floating islands. Nausea rose in David's gut. He'd seen this before. The island they stood on, which they tore chunks of flesh from, was no doubt a corpse. Human or animal, he didn't want to know. With his binoculars, he scanned the southern horizon. Only the Victoria Point tower remained, though there wasn't much left of what was once a beautiful apartment building, with a crest on top like a cockatoo. David remembered how the sunset used to turn the building gold. Now, most of the glass had been smashed, torn out in the wave, or in the gale-force winds since.

Some buildings collapsed under the weight of tonnes of concrete on buckled and busted frames, and others disintegrated from the inside, leaving only a skeleton reaching out above the sea. David shuddered—there were already enough skeletons under the waves.

CHAPTER FOUR

Emma entered the mess hall; a small, repurposed hangar with flyscreen covering the entrance allowing the scent of the sea to commingle with the earthy aroma of coffee. Private Patersall, whose piercing blue eyes made Emma's skin crawl, turned away when he saw her. *Thought so, creep.*

She hadn't been surprised when all the bread and fresh milk had disappeared. The upper echelon of the Defence Force probably had decent food, but the rank and file? No way. The local grain stores had been flooded, and thousands of animals were killed by the tsunami or died in the chaotic weeks of darkness afterward. Desperate times called for desperate measures, so she spread a thin layer of vegemite across three Weet-

Bix biscuits, poured herself a black coffee, and sat down.

That was the other benefit of signing up with the ADF—you didn't have to worry about where your meals were going to come from.

***

The patrol consisted of Emma, Corporal Nelson, Lance-Corporal Basada, and Privates Patersall and Fulham. Their mission, as usual, was to keep the peace; stop looters, break up fights, and get 'volunteers' for the labour camps.

Under dark clouds they crossed the Calder Freeway on foot, picking their way through the ruined cars, trucks, and buses. Most of the corpses had been removed from the wrecks and burned, but the vehicles remained, jutting out from the highway like gravestones.

The patrol walked in single file down a street lined with once respectable single-level family homes. Several still stood, but most had collapsed outright or were missing walls. The streets throughout the suburb were littered with debris and ash. An overturned tram, now forty tonnes of rust, had destroyed a dental clinic. A Red Rooster restaurant had been flattened by a fifty-metre fishing boat. Waves lapped against buildings just two hundred metres away and the cry of seagulls filled the salty air.

The residents close to the barracks were quiet, and mostly kept to themselves. Many homes were marked with crosses; tape on the windows or pieces of wood tied together. Emma didn't know if the crosses were to show support for Messinger or to indicate people had died there. She decided that she didn't want to know.

Her stomach tightened as they approached Moonee Ponds creek. One hundred metres wide and full of corpses, it couldn't be called a creek anymore. As they crossed, Emma pulled her shirt over her nose to block out the stench of salt water and rotting bodies. It didn't work. The horrific scent invaded her nostrils, making her gag, making her eyes water. She forced down her nausea and looked to the south, where the distant towers of the ruined CBD caught the sun's rays, shimmering silver and gold. It almost looked pretty through her blurry, tear-streaked vision.

A crudely written sign on the side of a building declared, 'DROWN THE HOMOS.' Fulham pointed it out to Patersall, his eyes bright with cruel mirth.

Patersall shook his head and held up his F88 Austeyr assault rifle with a knowing smile. "Why drown them? There are better ways."

The laughter of the squad chilled her to the core. Just six months ago, rainbow flags had been flown proudly throughout Melbourne. What had happened? How had attitudes swung so dramatically? The answer was all around her. The city had been struck by tragedy, and General Messinger has given them a scapegoat. All Emma could do was follow orders.

The patrol turned south down Sydney Road, once a thriving street lined with shops and restaurants. While thousands still slept in tents at the Tullamarine Airport, business had returned to Sydney Road. People had begun rebuilding the shops, selling salvaged or stolen supplies, all in hope the sea wouldn't rise any further.

Grunts and thuds echoed down an alley. Keen for action, Corporal Nelson signalled to the others. The patrol crept towards the sound of struggle, eyes peeled.

Emma's grip tightened on her assault rifle, her heart racing. Halfway down the alley, a man lay on his back in the mud, shirt torn, his mouth a mess of blood and broken teeth. Two assailants had trapped another man—thin and red-bearded—against a wall.

His attackers saw the patrol and sprinted away direction down the alley.

"Basada, Fulham, after them!" Nelson ordered. As they took off, Nelson eyed the man lying in the dirt, groaning in pain, and turned his M4 carbine on the man with the beard. "What's your story?"

"Those pricks attacked us . . ." He hesitated, his

voice quavering as he looked down the barrel of Corporal Nelson's assault rifle. "They jumped us out of nowhere."

"So who are you?" Nelson's grin made Emma's stomach squirm. She knew that smile.

"I'm Todd McCarthy, sir."

"Get on your knees, Todd."

"Why?" he pleaded. "I haven't done anything wrong."

"We know about you. About you and your *boyfriend*." Patersall said the final word with a sneer.

Todd's face went pale. "That's what this is about? For fuck's sake, so what if we're gay? We haven't hurt anyone."

"Haven't hurt anyone? Look around, ya faggot." Corporal Nelson's face was twisted into a snarl. "The Earth was flooded to get rid of your wretchedness, your filth. And what do you do? Go out and sin again."

"You can't seriously believe tha—"

Nelson's boot sank into Todd's stomach, cutting him short. Emma closed her eyes, feeling nausea well up inside her. She'd seen this before, been on too many patrols where Nelson and Patersall turned to violence—horrific, needless violence—against people trying to survive. People just like—

She shut down, detaching herself from the horror in front of her.

***

After Basada and Fulham returned empty-handed, the patrol returned to the barracks, Emma following a couple of metres behind.

"You did good today, Patersall," Nelson said to the young soldier. "If General Messinger hears about this, you might even get a promotion."

"Thanks Corporal," replied Patersall. "I'm just doing my job, doing my part to restore our city."

Emma felt sick. The bastards were proud of what they'd done. And the worst thing was Nelson was right, Messinger would probably reward their behaviour, not condemn it.

More than ever, she knew she had to get out.

***

Back at Essendon Fields, Emma had a couple of hours to kill before she was rostered on for food prep. Seething with quiet anger, she went to the gym to release it on padded bags and styrofoam. She was loathe to leave the privacy of the women's barracks, but she needed to do something, work out her anger, her pain. Her stomach in knots, she entered the dilapidated gym. Finding herself alone under the arched roof of the former aeroplane hangar, she breathed a sigh of relief. Dressed in a tank top and loose-fitting shorts, she walked to the nearest punching bag, positioning herself where she had a clear view of the door, to watch if anyone else came in.

Before long, she was pounding the punching bag with swift, powerful movements. *Left, left, right. Left right left. Left left right. Right right left. Nelson Patersall Nelson. Left left knee. Patersall Nelson Patersall. Left left left. Messinger Messinger Messinger. Right left knee. There has. To be. A better. Way.*

Exhausted, she braced her hands on her knees, sucking in lungfuls of air. *There must be a better way. But not here. Not while pigs like Messinger and Nelson are in command.*

"Don't see you in here much, Private Ramsey."

An icy chill pierced her stomach. *Shit.* She had to go. "Well I'm about to leave, so . . ." Emma turned around and Patersall was there, not even pretending to look her in the eye.

"So soon?" he said, a mock frown on his face.

"I'm rostered on at the chop shop in a bit, so yeah." She walked past him, feeling his eyes on her as she headed to the shower. She forced herself into a slow walk, hiding her panic, praying he wouldn't follow her. *This is why you never go to the gym alone, Emma.*

She turned down the hallway to the women's

shower and turned the tap on hot, filling the room with steam as she undressed, her heart racing. Not for the first time, she wished they had private shower cubicles. But no, not in this man's army. *Please don't come in, please don't come in.* Footsteps. Her heart thumped in her chest. The creak of the door swinging open. *Fuck.*

"Ramsey, where are you?"

She didn't answer. The steam coming from the stall, the sound of rushing water on the rough concrete floor, answered for her.

"You know we shouldn't be wasting water." Patersall's naked chest appeared through the steam, his face contorted in a sick grin. *Fuck fuck fuck.*

Emma covered her chest with her arms. "Stay the hell away from me!"

"Come on, I got so worked up beating the crap out of those fags, I need a little stress relief."

"Not going to happen, Patersall," Emma growled, backing away in fear.

"I'm not going to give up that easy."

Fuck. What do I do? Fear and adrenaline running through her system, Emma stepped right underneath the shower head, watching Patersall. Like a dog after a treat, his eyes focused on her breasts as she raised her arms upwards, her heart racing, her hands searching, desperate. *There!*

"I want you so bad . . ." muttered Patersall, stepping forward. Stepping within range.

Emma directed a powerful blast of scalding water into Patersall's face.

As he took a step backwards, wiping his eyes, she stepped forward. This was her chance. Desperate, terrified, she kicked him between the legs. He dropped to his knees, and looked up at her, hatred plastered on his face. She lashed out with her left elbow, as hard as she could. Patersall's body lurched right, his head hitting the wall. Trembling, Emma shut off the water. Without drying off, without taking her eyes off Patersall's unconscious body, she got dressed. *So much for being safe in the Defence Force.* She hesitated, caught between going to Corporal Nelson, and running so far and fast that she would never come back. She stepped over the crumpled body on the floor, then took another step. Another step and she was running, running for safety.

Her legs were aching, her lungs burning, when she locked herself inside the empty women's barracks.

"Jo!" she cried to the friend she hadn't seen in weeks—a broken scream, a hoarse, cracked whisper. "I need you."

Alone, her hands shaking, Emma staggered to the bathroom and threw up. Faint thunder rumbled in the distance as she lay on the floor, trembling in fear and revulsion. A storm was going to hit, and Emma knew she had to find shelter.

CHAPTER FIVE

Returning home from their salvaging trip, David left Sal to sort out the mess of their collected ropes and chains. They had done well—better than David would have expected, all things considered.

While Sal sorted the ropes, David started the long journey upstairs with a bucket of sea water. His legs ached by the time he reached the rooftop, and he paused to catch his breath, watching the orange glow of the sunset over the horizon. The flashes of orange on the waves showed where his thriving bayside community used to be. All lost. Linda. Everything he had. The home they had made. Linda's vinyl collection. The '72 Valiant Charger he'd spent years restoring, years promising he'd get her running again.

Focusing on the future, David turned to the homemade desalination system, removed the tarpaulin, and poured the bucketful of seawater into the bathtub. He retrieved the quarter-full container of fresh water and poured it into their spare drink bottles, then returned the container to the centre of the tub. Pulling the tarp back over, he placed a rock in the middle—right above the fresh water container. When it was sunny, the salt water would humidify and collect on the tarpaulin, then drip into the container, leaving the salt behind. It was a good system, and he and Sal had rigged many of them up for their neighbours.

A row of pots, full of earth and hope, stood waiting for the next shower. Rooftops all over the city were covered in buckets to collect rainwater, David's desalination systems, and garden beds. No-one had grown anything edible yet, or if they had they were keeping it to themselves. Until then, they made do with whatever fish they could catch, whatever survived the wave, and whatever could be salvaged or traded for with the fishers from the mainland.

David gazed across at the other buildings, wondering how much longer it would take for their hard work to bear fruit. How long the community could live off fish, seaweed, and whatever they could salvage or trade for.

Looking towards the mainland, the dark water stretched on for kilometres. After all this time, he was still shocked to find the Carlton Gardens flooded—only the top of the Royal Exhibition Building emerged from the depths. Beyond the Exhibition building, rooftops of the taller buildings and commission housing were visible in the distance.

Very few of David's friends ventured that close to the mainland, to the vague border between their communities. *A no-man's-zone. No, a drowned-man's-zone.* Amongst those houses, still trapped in their cars, were bodies neither the mainlanders or city-dwellers had the time or resources to clean up.

***

When David and Sal reached Central Island, the other salvagers and city-dwellers were already pooling their assembled ropes and cables. Next to the pile, under the watchful eyes of the ever-present gulls, the community dinner was being prepared.

"What have you got for us?" asked Baker, extending his hand in welcome.

"A shit-load of rope." A proud grin crossed Sal's face.

When Baker showed them the pile that had already been gathered, Sal's mouth fell open. "I reckon we'll be able to tie all the city together with that!"

Kintha placed a coiled length of rope on the pile and nodded her approval to David. "Good haul today, guys."

"Thanks."

"How much did Hassan get?" Sal asked.

"More than half of what's there."

"Strewth."

David smiled—there was a friendly rivalry between them and Hassan, each trying to outdo the other, to bring the best stuff back to the community.

"Alright, I'm going to make sure they aren't burning all my fish," Kintha said, smiling. "I'll see you both later."

"See you!" David called after her retreating figure.

Baker cleared his throat and drew David's eye. "I see the way you look at her . . ."

"What are you talking about?"

"You know."

David looked back at Kintha. She was pretty, but they both still wore wedding rings. He brushed his gold band with his thumb. Like his heart, the soft metal was dented and scarred. He wasn't ready. He didn't think he'd ever be ready. And her? Did she still hold onto hope her partner was alive out there? He turned back to the mass of ropes and helped Baker sort them into piles.

For dinner, they ate fish with a side of seaweed that had been dried out by Andretti, one of the oldest members of the community. David watched as Sal, sitting with Freya, Rafi and Gus, looked across to Andretti as he wrapped a piece of seaweed around his fish and took a bite. Sal hated the seaweed, but smiled at the old woman as he chewed, acknowledging her contribution. As she turned away, he slid the remaining pieces through a gap between the wooden panels that made up Central Island.

As the last bite was eaten, the community applauded the cooks, the fishers and Andretti for the meal, before turning their attention to the radio for Messinger's weekly announcement.

"Citizens of Melbourne—do not lose hope," Messinger began, his voice crackling over the static. "We have survived the wave. And we are rebuilding our lives, rebuilding the city. Today, our crews have cleared the last section of the roads connecting our Simpson Barracks to the Northern Hospital, and another section of the Maroondah Highway."

"Ugh, who needs stupid roads?" Freya asked. Salim and the rest of the kids laughed, and David couldn't help smiling.

"The clearing of these roads is vital to allow

supplies to reach us. We all have a role to play in rebuilding our society." His tone changed. "But there are some amongst us who are not playing their part, who are making it hard for the ADF to do their job. I'm talking about the parasites who live in the ruins of the old city."

A sharp intake of breath echoed through the community.

"I've been told these people have been sneaking to the mainland at night, stealing our supplies. Stealing your food. Your children's food."

"What the hell?" Elise said, enraged.

"What's he talking about?" Salim asked.

"He's lying. We aren't goddamn thieves."

"Why would he lie?" Corinne asked. "Why would he blame us?"

Alfred shook his head. "It's a diversion. Maybe the mainlanders are getting sick of him. Maybe there's a food shortage, and he's wanting to point the finger at someone else."

"What can we do?"

"Nothing. Wait and see how this plays out."

Angry voices spread across the island, drowning out the rest of the broadcast. From the midst of the voices came a soft song. Kintha, as she often did, was singing a gentle melody against the anger. David strained, trying to catch the lyrics, then smiled in recognition. *My*

Island Home, of course. He raised his voice and sang along, joining the chorus until everyone on the island had a smile on their face. This community was their home, a place where they had found a purpose, family and sanctuary. Under the stars, their spirits lifted, they relaxed, sang more songs, and planned out which buildings they'd try to connect.

When the thunder echoed through the buildings and flashes of lightning lit up the sky, they scurried home, racing against the impending downpour. They would survive this storm, and had hope for tomorrow.

CHAPTER SIX

Emma rolled off her pillow, wet with salt water. No-one had come for her. Not Patersall, not Nelson, not even Messinger himself. Shaken and nauseous, she put on her uniform and gathered her strength. She forced herself to get ready to go to the kitchen for food prep duty. Work. Work was the answer. Occupying herself would occupy her mind, stop her from thinking about what could have happened, what had happened.

Carrots and potatoes—the only fresh vegetables they had. The only crops that weren't too badly affected by the weeks of darkness following Jagannatha's impact. Throughout Emma's shift, chopping up carrots and potatoes, her anxiety and nausea kept threatening to overwhelm her, in anticipation of being summoned to the commanding officer's quarters. *Crap.* Patersall would have already gotten in Nelson's ear, telling him some bullshit story. She shuddered, there was no way this wasn't going to end horribly.

When it was her turn to eat, she sat alone, keeping her back to the wall, too nervous to keep anything down. The other soldiers looking at her, some staring in outright hostility. *They knew.* They knew what Patersall had done. And what she had done, fighting him off, hurting him. And Patersall—their friend, their brother—would want revenge. That's how the world worked. That's why you didn't fight back.

She had two major problems—she couldn't fight the goddamn army, and she had nowhere to run to. Again, she thought of her family. She wanted to see them more than ever, wanted nothing more than to feel the security of her mother's embrace. But the treacherous distance between them, full of raiders and looters, scared her just as much as staying where she was. And that was if she even made it out of the city. Defence Force deserters were sent straight to the labour camps, dealt with severely by the heavy-handed and brutal security division. No, she would have to stay—for now, at least.

***

Another hour passed with no summons, with no superior officer even giving her a second glance. *What was happening? Why hadn't they come for her?*

Emma went to bed with her heart racing, still expecting the call at any moment. The wind whipped through the barracks, bringing the salty smell of the dark and angry ocean. As she lay in her bed, she listened to the low rumble of thunder and the waves in the distance. When she closed her eyes, she relived the fear of Patersall approaching her, naked and helpless, lust and violence in his eyes. She remembered the feeling of her leg, her elbow smashing into his body, the brief power which faded all too soon. *Where had that strength come from?*

Flashes of lightning lit up the room, the roll of thunder echoed through the night, and Emma's fear wouldn't leave her alone. Even now, at zero-three-hundred, Corporal Nelson could burst into her room—he had keys to all the locks. Or maybe even Messinger himself. *Maybe that's what was taking so long, maybe Messinger was travelling to Essendon Fields from the Simpson barracks. And would he believe her story?*

No matter what happened, Patersall would want revenge. Or any number of testosterone-filled jerks at the barracks might want to avenge their emasculated friend. This wasn't over. They weren't going to let her off this easy.

She remembered her life before Jagannatha. Of the men who had come into her life and found fresh ways to ruin it. *Are men always going to be so shit?* She thought of Gavin, her boyfriend when the wave came through.

"It'll be better when I'm done with the drink," he always told her. But the drink was never done with him and now it had taken him forever. For that, at least, she was grateful. *Why did I stay with that arsehole so long?* She asked herself for the seven thousandth time. He was rough with her, especially when he'd been drinking. Every time he went too far, every time he got too rough, he promised her "never again." And she believed him. The first five times. *Would I have ever left him?*

She sobbed into her pillow, knowing the answer. Whenever she tried to leave, she'd always baulked at the last minute, thinking about how he needed her. About how he might get better. How she might be able to convince him to go back to AA. She shuddered, remembering the violence, the fear. *Endless violence. Ebbing and flowing like the tides. And she was constantly caught in the middle of it. Even now. Especially now.*

As rain drummed on the roof of the hangar and thunder illuminated the emptiness, Emma wished Private Josephine Avery was here with her, that she wasn't so alone. She needed a friend more than ever. And Jo wasn't just her friend; she was radiant, funny and her very presence put Emma in a better mood. She couldn't quite explain it. No-one had made her feel so at ease since. . .

Emma forced her attention back to the present. Six months after the disaster, she was as unsafe as ever. And the women on the other side of the fence. . . *Is it always going to be like this?* Hot tears welled behind her eyes again at the hopelessness of her situation. *Am I always going to be a goddamn victim?* She didn't want to be. She wanted to be strong and independent. But she couldn't see any way out, any future where she wasn't living in fear.

CHAPTER SEVEN

"What's happening today, Da?" asked Salim as the morning sun shone into the office building, all traces of last night's storm gone.

"Do you want to go help build those rope ladders?" David rubbed his tired eyes.

"Sure."

"Come on, let's get to it. But coffee first."

The previous occupants had left the office well stocked with instant coffee and sugar, but David knew that it wouldn't last forever. Still, a coffee in the morning gave him some sense of normality while it lasted. He'd salvaged the gas burner from a wrecked yacht and had traded a pot plant to Corinne for a gas cylinder a couple of months ago. David smiled as he remembered how she'd given them the cylinder for nothing and wouldn't take no for an answer. The next day Sal took her a pot plant as payment, with a can of diced tomatoes hidden in the earth.

As the rich aroma of coffee filled the room, David was thankful that he and Sal had found this community. They didn't have much, but they shared what they had and worked together with hope, with respect and with love.

***

After refilling the desal system, David and Sal rugged up against the morning chill and rowed to Central Island under a cloudy sky. The sea was always full of rubbish, but the storms brought even more. As they negotiated the waves, David knew Sal was watching the rough surface for anything they could use.

"Glad you could make it!" Corinne gave them a smile before helping David and Salim out of their boat onto the wooden platform. Ivy was sitting nearby, playing with some toys that had been found in an abandoned apartment.

"How are you doing today?" David asked. Corinne had been on edge since the hotel came down—

they all had.

"I'm feeling better, thanks. Last night's sing-a-long was just the tonic."

David smiled, thinking of Kintha's face, shining as she sang.

"Shame it was cut short by the storm," said Sal, already looking for his friends amongst the crowd.

"Still, this community is special," said Corinne, "the way we support each other. I can't imagine having to look after Ivy alone on the mainland." She shook her head. "Elise was right, there are more dangers there."

"Nowhere's safe," David said. "At least here we know what our dangers are, and with these bridges and rope ladders, we might make our city even safer."

Corinne's long brown hair bobbed as she nodded. "Oh, we've got some new folks in town." With a flowing gesture, she indicated where Elise was talking to two men, one with a short red beard and a broader man with brown hair. Both looked bruised and beaten.

"Shit—did they come in the storm last night?" Sal asked.

"Looks like."

With a quick wave to Ivy, David and Sal walked over to meet the new arrivals.

"This is David and Salim," Elise introduced them with a smile. "Guys, meet Todd and Martin."

"Sal and I live in the old Origin Energy building," said David. "Up near the Carlton Gardens. We're salvagers, mostly."

"We're—well, I *was* a nurse," said Todd. "And Martin was a real estate agent. I don't know what we are anymore."

"You're safe." Elise smiled. "That's the important thing."

Relieved smiles crossed their faces.

"Are you good at cooking?" Sal asked, ever hopeful.

"Sal, don't ask them that!" Elise laughed. "We don't want them to head back to the mainland!"

"It's okay. There's nothing that would make us go back there." Martin squeezed Todd's hand.

"Well, you can stay with us as long as you like," said Elise. "You can settle yourselves in any uninhabited apartment or hotel room. Or, like Dave, you can live in an office."

"When you've settled in, let me know and Sal and I will fix you up with a desal system," offered David.

"That's nice of you. Are you some kind of technological genius?"

"He's no genius, don't worry about that!" Sal laughed.

"We all help each other out around here. I'm

pretty good with my hands, and I know some basic science."

"How did you get across in the storm last night?" asked Sal.

Todd and Martin looked at each other, exhaustion clear in their faces. "If it's okay, I think we'd just like to rest first."

"That's fine," said Elise. "Most nights we all meet up here and share a meal. If you like, you can meet the rest of us and tell us your story then. Save you having to repeat it over and over."

"Yeah, we might do that." Todd squeezed Martin's hand. "Anyway, good to meet you."

"Nice to meet you too."

***

David looked over the curved tenth-level balcony of the Wesley building, an ultra-modern office that had been built next to the Wesley church on Lonsdale Street. The pointed spire of the hundred-year-old church stood defiant against the waves twenty metres below—an iron grey finger raised, unbowed, against the surging water. *Where is God now?* David thought. *How could he have allowed this to happen?*

In the cold light of day, it became clear that

connecting all the buildings in the CBD with rope bridges was not going to work. They would have to throw the rope from building to building, and many were too far apart to make it possible.

But Sal, Gus and Rafi had come up with a plan. It was only ten metres from David and Sal's office to the nearby EastEnd apartment complex. From there, twenty metres to the Wesley building, and another ten to the Marriott Hotel on Exhibition Street.

They had worked hard throughout the whole day. All the cables and ropes had been connected from window to window, two at the top to hold onto, and a thick cable at the bottom. David and Baker were going back between the buildings, tightening all the bolts and checking all the knots. Even leaning over the side of the building to check the bolts made David feel nauseous. The idea of using one of those bridges—being suspended thirty metres above the angry, vengeful sea—sent chills up his spine.

Salim and the others—Freya, Gus and Rafi—had grown bored of building the bridges and were already dangling precariously over the waves, their small hands gripping the rope tight, trying to outdo each other by travelling the furthest. David watched with trepidation as the teenagers played.

"Da, we're going back to ours now, okay?" Salim

asked.

"In whose boat?"

"What d'ya mean?" said Sal, grinning. "We don't need no boats. Gus, Rafi an' me will take the bridge!"

"You're kidding, Sal!"

"We can do it! Why'd we bother making it if we ain't gonna use it?"

"It's for emergencies."

"But how will we know if it works in emergencies if we can't try it now?"

David knew these kids. They were going to try the bridges, no matter what he said.

He sat in his boat, watching the three tiny figures inch their way along the rope bridge between the Wesley building and the EastEnd apartments, twenty metres in the air. The sea was calm, the tide receding. Out of habit, he peered over the side. Not five metres below him was the ruin of a building, concrete pillars, glass panels. He turned away. More than once he'd seen a face look up at him from beneath that glass, a face he knew too well.

The bright, fearless laugh of youth echoed off the buildings. David looked up at Salim and his friends. They were making good speed and has crossed almost halfway to the next building.

David rowed after them, navigating between the ruins, negotiating the waves. A scream from above. One of the figures—David couldn't make out who—was dangling by one arm from the rope bridge. *Shit.* A sick pit of fear opened up inside him. David rowed as fast as he could towards where the kid was hanging. To where the kid was falling.

A sickening splash and David cursed himself for not being closer, for not paying more attention. *Dammit!*

"Help, Da!" came Salim's plea. A wave of relief filled him. If he could hear Sal, Sal couldn't be underwater.

He rowed on, fear and guilt powering him. *I should never have let them cross.* How long had the kid been under? Twenty seconds?

"Where is he?" David cried.

"Just there," came the call from above, "to your right!"

David looked out of the boat—nothing. Falling from twenty metres, they would have gone ten metres under. David couldn't see anything through the dark turbulent water, but he knew the ruins—concrete slabs, steel pillars—were there. "Here? Are you sure?" He couldn't hide the tremor in his voice.

"Yeah."

David dived into the freezing water.

His jeans and his shirt weighed him down. He opened his eyes and a dark shadow appeared ahead of him. *Oh no.* He swam closer, the sea water stinging his eyes.

It wasn't a shadow.

Blood was mingling with the water, turning it dark. In a panic, he followed the cloud of blood.

The kid was impaled through the chest by a steel pole that poked up from the ruins like a shaft of anger. David recognised the face. Rafi. His mouth was open in a horrific scream of agony, a scream which would echo forever under the sea.

CHAPTER EIGHT

Emma was all alone in the crowded mess, eating her vegemite on Weet-Bix breakfast, when Private Josephine Avery entered. Her battered heart lifted—it had been weeks since she'd last seen her friend, and right now she needed Jo more than ever.

"Jo!" She got to her feet, embracing her friend in a tight hug, felt her warmth, the tickle of her curly red hair against her cheek, and smiled. "What—what are you doing here? How's Ferntree Gully?"

"It's a nightmare." Josephine cast an envious glance at Emma's breakfast. "We're understaffed and underfed, and our lock-up is overflowing."

Emma offered Jo the last of her Weet-Bix.

She shook her head. "That's why I'm here. Transporting non-critical prisoners and civilians here for treatment."

"I wish you could come back permanently. I miss you."

"Me too. I put in a request to be transferred back, but you know what they say. We go where we are needed, and that puts me up to my neck in shit. So how's it been here?"

Emma grimaced. She wanted to tell her friend about Patersall, but not here. "The Rydges hotel on Elizabeth collapsed a couple of nights back. It was a mess. We rescued some survivors, but . . ."

"I don't know how you can do it," Private Avery said. "Being out on the water near those buildings would give me the creeps. Amongst those people, amongst all that death. But listen, it's rough out east. I thought Sydney Road was bad, but . . ." Jo shrugged. "I'd normally want you to transfer there, but . . . They hate us out there. I mean, no-one's done anything, but I can feel it. It's tense, the way they watch us, the way the prisoners speak to us, refuse their orders."

"I'm scared here too, Jo," Emma whispered.

They sat in silence for a minute before the PA

speakers crackled to life. "This is Captain Rynard. All available personnel, report to the Parade Ground at oh-six-hundred. General Messinger is on his way."

Oh no. Panic and dread filled Emma's stomach. *He's coming for me.*

Jo stood up. "I should get going," she said, pausing as she saw the look on Emma's face. "Are you okay?"

"I'll be fine," Emma lied, forcing a nervous smile. "Come back sometime, okay?"

Jo nodded. "Hopefully they accept my transfer request, but . . ." She shrugged.

Emma understood. *We go where we're needed.* Now Messinger was needed here, and Emma was terrified as to the reason why.

***

"We are the lucky ones, spared from the wrath of the Almighty," Messinger preached from his platform as Emma stood to attention in the rain.

Months ago, when the clouds lifted after weeks of darkness, Emma had agreed with him. She wanted to believe God had saved her for a reason and given her a purpose. But now she had her doubts.

"God sought to spare us, so he could use us to rebuild the world, his way."

More like Messinger's way.

"We are constantly losing resources to those sewer rats in the drowned city. You know who they are. They're the blighted sinners that God sent the wave to wash away." Messinger paused, looking at the assembled soldiers from underneath his bushy grey eyebrows. "The homosexuals, the sinners, and the socialists afraid of doing an honest day's work. What are you doing about it?" he bellowed. "You're doing nothing, goddamn it!"

Emma stayed focused on the barbed wire fence bordering the barracks, hoping this would be over soon.

Messinger slammed his fist on the podium, his face red. "I always said if those homosexuals were allowed to marry, then the floodgates would open. And didn't they, by God?" Messinger raised his arms and gestured to the wreckage of the city. "Didn't they, by God?" he repeated, daring for anyone to disagree with this self-evident truth. "And now they're being held accountable, them and their bleeding heart red-flag waving enablers are turning tail and running, taking precious food, water and medicine. Our supplies, dammit! I want you to get our supplies back. And I want you to bring them back. Not only the ones who need medical treatment, not just when the buildings come down. I want you to bring every single one of those thieving bludgers to the shore."

This is new.

"I'm going to close off that city for good. Every single one of those drowned rats is going to return to the mainland and contribute to our society. Hell, it's their fault the Jagannatha came, the least they can do is help us red-blooded men clean up the mess and build the new world. And if they come quietly, they might only spend months in the labour camps to payback the hassle they've caused."

Oh God, really? Emma stared, horrified, as Messinger marched off the parade ground. Taking the survivors from the fallen towers—people who had nowhere else to go—was bad enough, but this?

"At ease," said Captain Rynard.

Emma glanced at her comrades and was met with eager faces, faces of determination.

"You're dismissed. You will be briefed on your new missions this afternoon."

Emma's heart sank. The Defence Force was hardly a force for good, and now they were going to drag every single person back to the mainland—the place they felt so threatened they had to run away from. To top it off, they were going to put them in labour camps to pay off some bullshit imagined debt. *Fuck.* If that's what Messinger's God wanted them to do, the city was beyond hope, beyond salvation. *Messinger doesn't follow the Christian God—he worships the God of Fear.* A void of hopelessness opened up inside her. *This was going to go swimmingly.*

***

Under the cover of darkness, Emma sat in the stern of a speedboat with Nelson, Basada, Fulham and Patersall. They were targeting the buildings in the north-east of the city in a repatriation mission. Patersall sat opposite her, his fierce eyes boring in on hers. She shuddered under his hostile stare and looked toward the distant towers. He hadn't said a word to her, nor had Nelson. But with a cold certainty she was sure Nelson knew. And Patersall hadn't got so much as a slap on the wrist. Dread filled her soul. Sooner or later he would come for her again. Emma gripped her F88 assault rifle, comforted by its presence. She could—*would*—use it if she had to. The rough water was dark and foreboding, the ruined buildings they swerved around were desolate and abandoned. She was always nervous when on a mission, but never like this. Something bad was going to happen.

Something catastrophic.

Emma had joined the ADF to help the people who had lost everything, to help the victims of the flood. *Who was going to help the victims of the ADF?* Revulsion and fear knotted in her stomach, working its way up inside her.

The sky was heavy with much-needed rain, and they'd cut their engines for a surprise raid. They were instructed to sneak into an apartment building, work their way up level by level, and capture who they could. Then they'd go out again and again, until *all the flea-ridden dirty scavengers had been rounded up.* Nelson's words.

Emma was sick with dread, but the other soldiers were keen for a fight. She thought she might be able to reason with these city-dwellers, she might be able to get a few of them to come willingly. But Nelson and Patersall were full of misplaced anger, and all the men liked shoving their weight around. A dangerous combination. *I have to get out of here. There's nowhere to go.* Her world had become a nightmare of impossible proportions, crashing like a wave through a city—unstoppable, brutal, and utterly ruinous.

CHAPTER NINE

David couldn't sleep. Every time he closed his eyes, he was underwater again, searching for Rafi. His body shook and he felt nauseous, full of despair and grief. Instead of sleeping, he stared at the ceiling, hearing the wind howl through the open window, the cries of the gulls and the waves against the side of the building.

The one thing he couldn't hear was Salim's deep, steady breathing from across the office.

"Sal!" he whispered. Nothing.

Sliding out of bed, David walked across to the side of the building that Sal had made his own. The moonlight illuminated an empty bed. But where could he have gone? Sal knew better than to take a boat . . .

Too late, David realised that while he struggled with the burden of not being able to save Rafi, Salim was grieving for his friend. And now that the building was connected by cables, Sal could explore, search for solace, and grieve in his own way, with his own friends.

David clambered up to the seventh floor where the rope bridge connected their office to the abandoned EastEnd building. Salim's torch was by the window. David felt a moment of fear—what if he falls, too? He hoped that Sal was wearing one of the rope harnesses Alfred and Hassan had devised after news of Rafi's death reached them. Of course, the fall itself wasn't dangerous. It was the ruins that lay only a few metres beneath the surface, hidden by the waves, that were lethal.

David sat, dangling his legs out the window, watching the curve of the rope leading into the darkness. Most of their neighbours lived in the surviving hotels and apartment complexes—arguably more comfortable than an office—but David had never liked hotels. He didn't like how by-and-large they were all the same. Living in someone else's apartment didn't appeal to him either. Taking over someone's home and going through their possessions didn't sit well with him at all. And there was always the one-in-a-million chance the owners would come back.

He'd turned to the city because his house, his life, was gone forever. He didn't want to spend months living in a tent city at the airport, in the slums without names. He didn't have a life he wanted to rebuild. He was an experienced diver, all he needed was a boat, a wetsuit, and a place to work—and he'd found all that in the submerged city. Now, hearing reports of the violence and fear which plagued the mainland, he was content with his decision. He'd already turned the lower floors into his workshop, and living above his workshop suited him, given how much work there was to do.

The moon was hidden behind clouds, but the outlines of the city's surviving buildings were still visible. Out there, the teenagers were now able to do what kids had always done, what he himself had done many years ago—sneak out of the confines of their homes and seek their own truth, their own adventures.

With a sigh, David looked out into the night, thinking of his youth—the nights he snuck out of his parents' home as a teenager, the nights he explored under the stars with his friends, stealing cars, talking about girls. They had talked about the future, about how they were going to change the world. What would his friends think of him now, working hard every day to change the world back to what it was? That's what he was doing, after all. Every day he dredged up pieces of the past, bringing whatever he could of the old world into the new one, trying to bridge the irrevocable chasm between them. Still, he hadn't changed the world. It was the world that had changed him. Yet, this bridge he had helped make, from cables and chains he had salvaged—it was not just a way of getting from building to building. These bridges allowed the kids to complete the time-honoured traditions of youth. They were one tentative step closer to how things had been. Together, David and the people of this community were restoring normality.

David stood up to return to bed and noticed a beam of light where a nearby apartment complex met the sea. *Who'd be out on the water this late?* David focused on the waterline. A dark boat was tied against the building. His heart lurched. An ADF speedboat. *What were they doing here?* As he watched, three dark figures climbed in through a window.

Heart racing, David ran up the stairs to the rooftop where they stowed a flare gun. Red for ADF. Green for natural disasters. Another question came to him with each floor he scaled. *Why were the Militia there? Had another building come down? But no—they had docked on an existing building. What was happening?*

His chest was burning, his legs aching, when he emerged from the stairwell into the wind. Grabbing the flare gun from the waterproof container, he fired up into the sky.

Three . . .

Two . . .

A vivid red light lit up the sky.

David stopped on each floor on the way back down, yelling for Salim, hoping that his son was still somewhere in their building. His voice was hoarse and broken when he returned alone to the seventh floor window.

CHAPTER TEN

Under the cover of darkness, Emma followed Corporal Nelson into the Marriott building, wading through knee-high water to the stairwell. Even the next floor up the carpet was damp. The place stank of the sea. And there was another odour, too.

"Cat piss," Fulham said, ascending the stairs behind her. "What do you think, Corporal?"

"I'm wishing the elevators still worked." Patersall's very presence made sickness rise inside Emma, his words filled her with disgust.

"If there's a cat still alive in here," said Nelson, "some faggot must be feeding it. Let's spread out and search this floor. You see something, you say something."

Emma turned to the north while her comrades stomped down the hall to explore the other rooms. The door in front of her had been flung wide, clothes and trinkets scattered across the floor. Moonlight shone through the window on an unmade bed. Everything was tatty, lumpy or wrinkled. Her torchlight illuminated the room, but nothing stirred.

Please let this apartment be empty. Please let this whole building be empty. Letting that arsehole Messinger down was far more preferable than betraying other people who just wanted to get on with their lives.

Pain shot up her right leg. "Shit!" she exclaimed, falling onto the damp carpet with a squelch. Her heart raced in the silence.

"Ramsey, are you okay?" Basada's voice echoed down the hall.

Emma shone her torch around, looking for an assailant. The room was a mess, but empty. At her feet was a low coffee table. "Lance-Corporal, I tripped over a table. I'm okay."

"Jesus, Ramsey. Get your shit together."

Emma got to her feet, gritting her teeth. She'd have a bruise tomorrow, but nothing to write home about.

Her torch beam shone through rows of plastic bottles stacked on the kitchen bench, some still half-full. A shadow jumped into the light, a small black-and-white shape. A cat. Emma followed it, her footsteps accompanied by the soft jingling of bells, until the cat reached an empty food bowl and looked at her, its yellow eyes pleading. The cat's attention shifted to the corner of the room, and Emma's beam followed.

"Footsteps upstairs—everybody on the double!" Nelson' voice echoed down the hall as Emma's torch fell upon a shape cowering in the corner.

Her heart raced.

A pale face, eyes hidden behind a mop of dark unkempt hair. Eyes full of fear.

She swallowed, taking a hesitant step backwards. She knew she should call out—her orders were to alert Corporal Nelson and her squadmates—but something stopped her.

"Ramsey? Are you coming?" Basada called from the hall.

She backed out of the kitchen, her index finger pressed to her lips.

***

As she climbed to the next floor, Emma heard the footsteps that had drawn Nelson's attention. Emma's heart sank into the dark ocean. *Would these people even defend themselves? Could they?*

"We've got contact. Fourth floor up." Nelson radioed to the second squad as Basada's torch lit the hall. They listened for any sound, looked for any movement, any light. The second-last door was open, just a crack. Corporal Nelson nodded, and Fulham pushed it open. Torchlight fanned the room. Piles of old newspapers and clothes were strewn across the floor. Rows of empty plastic bottles. Someone had been living here. They stepped into the room, rifles at the ready. Next to a dead TV was another door—closed.

This door was like any of the millions of doors Emma had seen in her twenty-seven years. But she knew going through this door, crossing this threshold, would change her.

"Kick it down, Ramsey." Nelson's voice was cold steel.

Emma took a deep breath, focused and jumped, kicking out with her right foot, encased in steel and leather. A scream rang out, and Fulham and Patersall burst through the door, assault rifles raised.

Cowering against the far wall was a woman—a

bundle of rags and messy dark hair—already on her knees begging to be spared.

Emma realised the woman had been through this before. Maybe decades ago, maybe in a far corner of the world. Her pain and fear were there, but beneath it all was an understanding, a resignation that broke Emma's heart.

Corporal Nelson kicked the woman in the stomach. "Where are the others?"

The woman shook her head, her hands pleading.

"Where is everyone, bitch?"

She answered, but in a tongue Emma didn't know.

"She doesn't understand," Fulham said.

"Well, make her understand," ordered Nelson.

"I don't speak whatever she speaks."

"God dammit, we don't have time for this!" Basada snapped.

"What are we going to do?" Patersall's finger was already on the trigger.

Nelson shook his head and readjusted his glasses. "Private Ramsey, take her to the boat. Cuff her if you need to."

Heart heavy, Emma reached her hand out to the woman. "Come with me."

No response.

Emma knelt down and took her hand. The woman flinched at her touch and looked up into Emma's eyes. Not knowing what else to do, she grabbed the woman by her thin wrists and pulled her to her feet, dragging her out of the room. Down and down they went, the woman hesitating at every step. By the time they reached the lowest floor, hurried footsteps echoed down the stairs behind them.

"Prepare the boat, Private!" Nelson's voice echoed down the stairwell.

When Emma reached the boat, the glow of a red flare was reflected in the choppy water. "They've seen us, Corporal!" she shouted up the stairwell. "The whole sky's lit up."

Basada drew nearer to Emma, leading a handcuffed figure, and Fulham was dragging something behind him, thump, thump, thump down the stairs.

Emma stepped into the boat, holding it steady for the elderly woman, not letting go of her wrist. The woman was shaking in fear as she collapsed into the bottom of the boat, a soft whimpering coming from the pile of rags.

"Get into the boat, kid," Basada growled to his denim-clad prisoner.

He couldn't be older than seventeen. He crawled into the boat, hampered by his handcuffs.

Fulham grunted as he dumped a small figure wearing a dark green jumper into the back of the boat, causing it to rock. *Dead or—*

"What did you do to him?" asked Emma. She watched as the kid in denim turned to the dark-skinned kid in the green jumper and tried to rouse him.

"He's coming quietly now," said Patersall, grinning. "That's all you need to worry about."

"Captain Rynard's ordered us all back." Nelson wiped his glasses on his uniform, frustration plastered across his face. "That flare means we won't be taking anyone else by surprise. Fulham, cuff the old woman."

Emma turned away as Fulham pulled out his handcuffs and reached for the woman. She was happy the mission had been cut short but despaired for the people they had stolen from their homes.

With her heart aching, she watched the old woman struggle in her cuffs, shivering against the cold. The head of the unconscious kid lolled to the side with the movement of the boat as they took off and cut through the waves. Anger and disgust filled her as Nelson manoeuvred the speedboat between buildings, they had the chance to rebuild the world and make it better, but instead Messinger's hate and fear was tearing them all apart. It was as if the darkness they had been shrouded in after Jagannatha fell had seeped into their souls. Something needed to change.

***

Emma's chest was tight with dread as they approached the dock. The woman was confused, silently weeping. The handcuffed kid was looking at his captors, defiance in his eyes. The other kid was still unconscious. She'd always felt a pang of guilt when bringing people back from collapsed towers but could justify it as they'd had nowhere else to go. But this was something else.

As they prepared to dock, the young kid sprung to life, jumping over the side of the boat, landing with his arms outstretched on the ramshackle pontoon.

"Shit—get him!" Basada yelled.

"Ramsey—after him!" ordered Nelson.

Emma was out of the boat in a heartbeat, her legs pumping like pistons, but the kid was soon swallowed up by the darkness.

"Don't let him get away!"

"Run, Sal!" came the voice of the other kid from the boat. "Don't let them catch—"

The voice was cut short by a sickening crunch.

Emma's legs pounded underneath her as she ran down one alley and then another. She'd lost him.

And then a scrape, a scrabble up ahead—there!

"I'm not going to hurt you!" Emma called in a hushed whisper to the shadows.

Footsteps—he was running again. Straight towards the barracks.

"Not that way . . . Sal! Go east!" she called as loud as she dared.

A slight pause. The footsteps continued, no change in direction.

Emma had no time to think as her legs propelled her forward, through the shadows of half-demolished buildings. Then she saw him—a frightened figure caught in the moonlight, not sure which way to run.

Heart racing, Emma stopped, drew in a deep breath, and raised her arms in the air. "If you keep going that way, you'll run into the barracks."

"Why should I believe you?" he spat.

"I don't want you dead. I don't want you in the labour camps."

"I want to go home. I want to go back to the city. To my family."

Emma paused, stunned. "Family?" She'd thought

those living in the city were just riff-raff castaways. This kid had a whole family in those ruined buildings? *Crap.*

"Not blood family, but as close as you can get."

"Look," said Emma, "if you go back, we'll just come out and capture you and everyone else again. That's our orders."

"What kind of bullshit orders are they?"

Emma risked a glance over her shoulder. There was no-one near them yet, but they would catch up soon enough. "Listen to me. Get across the river and follow the coast east."

"Why?"

"Because this city's going to hell," she whispered. "And it's going to get a lot worse before it gets better."

"Private Ramsey? Where are you?"

Emma jumped and whirled around, searching for the source of the voice. When she turned back, the kid was gone.

"Here, Corporal. That sucker was fast."

"The idiot's running straight for the barracks," said Nelson, smiling as materialised out of the shadows. "I'll radio through and make sure they apprehend him."

An empty pit had opened up inside Emma, and Sal's frightened, bruised face stayed with her as she returned to Essendon Fields in silence. *Maybe I should have gone with him.*

CHAPTER ELEVEN

With his heart pounding in his chest, David stepped out onto the rope bridge, the rope harness tight around his waist. Dark waves crashed against the building several storeys below, the white crests visible in the blackness. The thin cable was almost invisible, and David felt that he was stepping out into nothingness and the great chasm beneath him would claim him any second. He forced himself to keep going—he had to find Salim. *What would Linda say?* He clenched his teeth and took another step into the darkness. His arms shaking, he moved his hand further down the cable and took another step. And another.

His foot slipped, his heart burst out of his chest as he fell, for a fraction of a second. But the ropes held.

With his muscles straining, his heart racing, David put his foot back on the cable. No-one else could help him, caught in the middle of the night between two buildings.

Covered in sweat, exhausted, David made it to the EastEnd building. He ran to the stairwell and shouted for Salim up and down the stairs.

He knew Salim wouldn't be there—it was too close to home to be any fun exploring, and besides, no-one lived there. But beyond stood the Marriott building where Gus lived, one of Sal's friends. The building where the ADF boats had docked.

His heart pounding, David went to the window where the bridge reached out to the next building. He paused, hoping to see Salim emerge from the darkness and make his way across to him.

The sound of faint voices above the crashing of the waves drifted up as he stood on the windowsill. Below, he caught movement. Figures were returning to the speedboat, their uniforms illuminated in the moonlight. Two figures huddled in the bottom of the boat, guarded by a woman with a pale ponytail. David held his breath as another figure was tossed into the boat.

A flash of dark green. *Oh no.* The roar of the speedboats starting told him he was too late.

Swallowing his fear, he stepped out into the darkness. There was a chance that it wasn't Sal who had been captured and thrown into the boat. He had to know for sure.

***

Calling out into the darkness of the Marriott hotel, David's heart leapt when footsteps echoed above him. "Sal?"

"David—there you are!" said Elise, her voice strained, as she came down the stairs.

"Have you seen Sal?"

"He's not with you?"

David shook his head, collapsing to the floor. "I saw the ADF boats from our building and fired off the flare. What were they doing here? What are *you* doing here?"

"I saw the sky light up, and their speedboat take off. I rowed across from the old Telstra office." She paused, concerned. "David, I think they've stepped up their operations and have started raiding us."

"Raiding us? What was taken?"

"Not what. Who. Andretti's gone. Gus too. You've heard how Messinger talks about us scumbag city parasites, stealing their supplies. He was preparing for this."

"Shit." David's stomach fell.

"Are you sure Sal's not in the Origin building?"

"Yes." David nodded. "I called out for him on every goddamn floor."

Elise tried to give him some hope to hold on to. "We won't know for sure until tomorrow when the sun's up and we've got decent light."

David groaned in frustration.

"Don't give up." Elise squatted next to him, scratching the back of her head through her closely cropped hair. "Sal's a tough kid. He'll be okay."

"And tomorrow?"

"Tomorrow we look for Sal and get ourselves ready for those bastards. If they come back, we'll be prepared. You did good with the flare gun, David. There wasn't anything else you could have done. Not without getting yourself captured, anyway."

As David sank into despair, knowing with a cold certainty that Sal wasn't going to show up tomorrow, footsteps echoed on the stairs below.

"David? Elise? Is that you?"

"Yeah, who's that?" Elise called into the darkness.

"Hassan." He climbed the stairs, a black-and-white cat in his arms.

"What happened?" David asked.

He shrugged. "They snuck up from the water level, came in armed to the teeth. Caught me by surprise. One of them came into my apartment, tripped over the coffee table."

"I hope the bastard broke his leg," Elise hissed. "So what, I guess they didn't see you?"

"No. She shone her torch right on me. But another soldier called out and they all ran upstairs."

"I don't get it." David scratched at his stubble. "Why would they leave you and take Gus, Sal, and Andretti."

"We don't know for sure they've taken Sal," Elise said. "But not much those bastards do makes any sense, does it?"

***

When the sky turned orange, heralding the new day, David got out of bed a broken man. He had hardly slept that night, hoping any noise was Salim returning, but in his heart he knew his adopted son, his friend, had been taken.

"How are you, David?" asked a familiar voice. Kintha sat by a window, sorrow in her eyes.

"What-what are you doing here?"

"I heard Sal was missing. I want to help—if there's anything I can do."

The mention of his name tore at David's heart. "Do you think he's still in the city somewhere?" His voice was a harsh rasp.

She shook her head. A slight movement, but enough to bounce her dark curls from side to side.

"So why are you here?"

"I thought you might need a friend. I care for you. For Sal."

"Well you want to know how I am? I'm shit. I thought my life couldn't have got worse after the wave swept everything away. But I was wrong. This is all my fault."

"Oh, Dave. No-one blames you for any of this."

"I do. I should have kept a better eye on him. Been a better dad."

Kintha turned to the window, giving David a moment with his pain. "Elise says they're going to come back."

A wave of fire, a wave of hate, burned through David. "When?" he asked, his voice cold.

"Maybe as early as tonight."

David nodded. The answer he had expected.

"If you want, I can help you search for Sal."

David shook his head. *If he was here, he'd have come back by now, or got a message to someone.*

"Well, if there's anything I can do, come find me. Alfred and Elise are planning our defence at Central." She got up and took a step towards the stairwell. When David didn't respond, she turned back to him. "You're not the only one who has a claim on the guilt here, David."

He watched as Kintha took a step towards him. *Will she take another? Will she try to cross this gap between us?*

"The rope bridges were my idea." Her voice shook.

David wanted to comfort her, but was drowning in his own pain.

"Without the bridges, Rafi wouldn't have fallen. Salim wouldn't have been at the Marriott . . ."

"Don't, Kintha," said David, gruffly. "The bridges were a great idea. Accidents happen. And it's no-one's fault if some arseholes from the mainland want to kidnap us."

Kintha sighed, made an aborted gesture with her hands. "You're right." Her voice betrayed guilt and pain she couldn't let go of. "I'll see you when you're ready."

CHAPTER TWELVE

Waking early, Private Ramsey put on her uniform and climbed to the top of the barrack's southern lookout tower, where the movements of the city-dwellers were monitored from. The early morning sea breeze restored her, if only a small amount. After acknowledging Sergeant Oliveri with a quick salute, she looked towards the ruined city.

Dark and foreboding, the towers stood out against the pale blue sky. Grey clouds were forming to the west—another storm on the horizon. Emma tried to remember the city's skyline—her city's skyline—from before the wave, before the darkness. She recalled days so far gone they must have been from a past life; when her family drove into the city to see football games and go on shopping trips. When her mum took her to see a band at Festival Hall and stayed in the car with a book while Emma and her friends enjoyed the show. Every single time they had cheered when they crested that last hill and caught a glimpse of the faraway city towers.

Recalling fond memories with her family, Emma wished she'd never signed on with the ADF. She wasn't helping. She wasn't where she needed to be. And she was on the verge of collapse.

The memories kept coming. She was too exhausted to stop them, to keep fighting them down. Emma remembered driving to Melbourne with Claire on a scorching hot day. How the old Holden station wagon—filled to bursting with clothes, doonas, CDs and crockery—didn't have air conditioning, and they'd hung their arms and legs out the windows. The awful shared house in North Melbourne. Those first few months of independence. How Claire had serenaded her in their room every night with her guitar, their delicate voices merging into one. She missed their short-lived, chaotic, passionate romance. Emma braced herself against the wall of the lookout tower, wracked with guilt. It had hurt her dad deeply when she and Claire had moved in together.

"I didn't raise you that way," he said. Six cold words down a phone line. His last words to her until she'd got together with Gavin. Even then, her dad's attitude hardly improved. There was a chasm between them still. No matter how much she tried to make things work with Gavin, how much she tried to forget those few months in North Melbourne, she couldn't bridge that gap between her and her father.

Looking out over the wreckage of what had once been, it all came flooding back. How they broke up because she'd been too scared to come out, unwilling to introduce Claire as anything more than her friend. Claire's last words, *"Come find me when your cowardice has stopped running your life,"* had stung. A fist of disgust hit her in the stomach as she realised she was still a coward. She had been too scared to stand up to Gavin. Too scared to leave the Defence Force. Too scared to admit—even to herself—that she was attracted to women. A solitary tear crept, unbidden, from her eye.

She focused on the buildings. The concrete monstrosity of 120 Collins was gone, and so was the Rialto. Most of the Southbank and Docklands skyscrapers, being hit hardest by the wave, had been wiped from existence. Thirty, maybe fifty percent of the buildings had been destroyed. And of those that remained, who knew how long they would last? It was only a few nights ago the Rydges hotel had collapsed.

"What are you thinkin', Private?" asked Sergeant Oliveri.

"Just wondering how long the rest of those buildings will last, Sergeant."

"Heard about the mission last night." He grinned, showing chipped, yellow teeth. "Reckon them buildings coming down is the best shot you've got of bringing those folk back to shore."

Emma reeled, recalling the disaster, that kid's face. "We'll get them, don't you worry." She felt sick to her stomach as the words left her mouth.

"Going back out tonight?"

"Affirmative."

"Glad it's you and not me."

She looked into his eyes.

"I know orders is orders . . ." Oliveri shrugged, then caught himself.

Emma's mouth hung open. *He was going to say it. He was going to say some orders shouldn't be followed.*

"My mum was a Christian. Always went to church—not that it did her any good—but she always said us Christians should turn the other cheek, treat everyone nice, treat everyone the same. Now, I'm no bible-basher, but I think the same."

Emma stood in silence, not knowing how to respond. She should report him for questioning Messinger's orders. But right away, she knew she couldn't. Oliveri might be one of the only other soldiers in the barracks—hell, in the entire army—with not just a brain, but a heart.

Oliveri stepped forward, a stern look on his face. "As you were, Private. This conversation never happened."

Turning her face away, she looked out once more to the skyline, now glowing with the reflection of the early morning sun. She did not want to go back out. Not tonight. Not any other night. But how could she get out of it?

***

Emma went to the mess, where she had just enough time to get a coffee before assembling for the daily patrol. The conversation with Oliveri was fresh in her mind, how he'd dared to question Messinger's orders. She and Jo had spent hours in the secluded women's barracks whispering about how bullshit it was, but it was a shock to learn others shared the sentiment. Whatever happened, she wasn't going to breathe a word of what Oliveri had said to anyone.

Her thoughts drifted back to Claire. Was it too much to hope that Claire had survived the wave, survived the days of darkness and despair? *Of course.* She couldn't afford to fantasise about rekindling an old flame. Especially with the people in power spreading hate and violence against the LGBTI community. *Maybe it's good I never came out.* She quashed the idea almost as soon as it appeared, bile rising in her throat. Emma couldn't afford to think about anything more than staying alive, finding a way out of this nightmare life, finding a way to stop her squad kidnapping any more people.

She sighed, defeated. Both her fantasy and her reality seemed equally impossible.

CHAPTER THIRTEEN

After returning from Central Island and assuring Elise, Baker and Alfred he was all right, David tried to sleep. It was only mid-afternoon, but he was exhausted from guilt and worry. He lay on his mattress in the too-silent office building, looking up at the long-dead fluorescent lights in the ceiling. Sal was gone. Probably transferred to one of the militia's labour camps, forced to work.

David remembered the first time a building had come down—the modern gold and copper building that used to tower above the old Melbourne Gaol. He had looked out the window with Sal, watching in horror as Messinger's Militia filled their speedboats with the injured.

"How come they're taking them back to the mainland, Da?"

"I don't know. Nothing that those arseholes do makes any sense to me anymore."

Sal's eyes gazed up into his own "Promise you'll come get me if they take me away?"

The kid had already been through so much, lost so much. It had hurt David's heart to imagine him being taken away. "Don't worry. You're too smart to let them catch you. But if they do, you know I'll go after you. It's what family does."

David rolled over, the memory sending shudders of grief through his body. Whenever he closed his eyes, Salim was there, screaming his name, crying for him to come and find him. Behind Sal stood Linda, her arms across her chest.

Linda. Her blue dress dripping with water, her hair floating around her face as if she was still underwater. *Of course she was.* Linda's dead eyes bored into his own, a silent accusation.

David struggled to breathe under the spectre's gaze. He should have done more to save Linda. He should have tried harder. And now Sal was gone, taken by the militia. To keep his promise to Salim, David would have to take on Messinger's army. A hopeless, impossible mission. He had no chance. He didn't even know where to start. David stared at the ceiling, torn between the impossibility of going after Sal and the agonising guilt of breaking another promise, of abandoning his son.

***

When David finally managed to fall asleep, things just got worse.

First, he dreamt he was underwater, scuba diving—but without his suit. He was submerged in the immense blackness and he couldn't breathe. A thin arm reached out for him far below.

He swam down, grabbed the arm and pulled. The soft decaying flesh gave way, sliding off the bone, leaving a skeletal arm and putrefying flesh in his hands. Nausea welled inside him, and he closed his eyes.

When he re-opened them, he was face-to-face with sunken death. The child's face was right in front of his own, big hollow holes where the eyes should have been, the mouth twisted into a scream.

David emerged from his nightmare shaken, covered in sweat, his throat on fire. Torn between the horror of his dreams and the despair of his waking life, he knew where his salvation lay.

He stood up, padding across the floor of the sunlit office to the stairs. He'd promised himself, of course, that he would never touch the alcohol that he'd found when he first explored the building—perhaps as a pathetic gesture to make amends with his past.

David had traded a couple of bottles of wine, but the good stuff—bottles of whisky, rum and vodka—he had buried inside the pot plants on the thirteenth floor. He couldn't touch them, or he'd break another promise, but he couldn't bring himself to part with them either. He'd kept them for special events—at least, that's what he told himself. One for Sal's eighteenth birthday, one for when the first child of their community was born.

But right now, he needed a drink. He needed whisky. The good stuff, the Japanese.

Each flight of steps was a new battle of wills. He was going to break another promise. But what was one more after so many over the years?

At each floor—each test of his strength—he failed, breaking through barrier after barrier to get closer to the alcohol. He needed a sip, just one sip to make everything better.

The late afternoon sun shone through the window of the thirteenth floor, bathing the office with a welcoming warmth. David dug his hands into the warm earth of the pot plants, searching for something to dull the pain. For something he could cling to, something he could believe in.

Hands trembling, he tore the lid off the bottle of Yamazaki Distiller's Reserve and took a long swig. The smooth burning liquor provided a moment of clarity that he so desperately sought.

"To Rafi." David took a shot and looked out the window towards where the boy had fallen, his gut churning. He poured himself another.

"To Sal."

David filled the glass one last time, then looked at his wedding ring. He couldn't bring himself to say her name aloud. *To Linda.*

He sat the half-empty bottle on a table and made his way back down the stairs. Elise was right—they needed to plan how to defend their community. And he needed to talk to her about Sal, if there was any way to get him back. David knew that Elise also ached for a chance to get revenge against the militia. Elise was a fighter. Not like Linda, not like Kintha, not like himself. She might be cold, but she was smart and radiated an inner strength, a confidence. At some point Elise had put her foot down and said, "No. You don't get to treat me like that."

Now that the mainland mongrel bastards had taken Sal—now that he'd lost everything—David was going to put his foot down too. *Right down their goddamn throats.*

CHAPTER FOURTEEN

Overcome with nausea, Emma emptied her stomach over the side of the speedboat.

"Private Ramsey," Basada sneered. "Get your shit together. We need this mission to be a success."

"I didn't think she got seasick," called Fulham from the boat behind them.

Emma shuddered, wanting to tell them it wasn't seasickness.

"The bitch has gotten herself pregnant," Patersall muttered, his eyes hostile.

Emma kept her mouth shut. The bristling anger helped her focus as she returned to her seat, picking up an oar.

"Will you be right for this mission, Private?" asked Nelson.

"Yes, Corporal!" Emma's eyes were glued to the towers where the city dwellers lived. She didn't want to be out here, to go on this mission, but she couldn't afford to show any more signs of weakness in front of the squad.

Emma shivered against the chill. They were approaching the city, the dark towers rising into the night sky. She scanned the buildings looking for light—the telltale sign of life—but there was nothing but darkness.

"What d'ya think, Corporal?" Basada whispered between oarstrokes.

Six boats were on the mission tonight, working in pairs. Captain Rynard was not going to tolerate any more fuck-ups. And neither was Messinger.

"They aren't going to make it easy for us," Nelson whispered back. "Now shut it and wait for my signal."

The air was thick with tension, fear and excitement. Emma felt Nelson's determination, his faith in his misguided duty. Her stomach squirmed under Patersall's hostile glare.

"There!" Fulham hissed. "10 o'clock."

Emma looked up into the buildings to the left,

her heart racing. Light. Two—no, three—windows were lit up in the one building, about halfway up. A moment later, they winked out.

"That's where they're hiding," Nelson smiled. "Now to find a way in."

In silence, they approached the dark tower. A loose window above the waterline gave them the access that they needed.

Nelson pulled himself through the window into the apartment with a splash. They all froze at the sound, and Basada hissed through his teeth.

Nelson turned towards the soldiers, careful not to make any more noise. He pointed at Fulham, and then at the boats. Fulham nodded and sat back down, reaching for the cigarette tucked behind his ear. Then Nelson indicated for Patersall, Ramsey, and Basada to climb through the window and follow him inside.

The hotel room was trashed and stank of rot. The floor, ankle-deep in water, was thick with clothes, ruined books and magazines. They waded through room after room in search of the stairs.

Basada tapped Nelson on the shoulder and gestured towards the stairwell. "How many floors, Corporal?" he whispered.

Nelson just shrugged and marched upwards.

With her heart sinking further every step she climbed, Emma followed along behind the men. They paused at each floor, listening for sound, looking for light—or any other clue—that their targets were there. At each floor, Emma prayed they wouldn't find anyone, that the light they had seen was simply a reflection from another building.

And then a sound. Footsteps above them. *Oh no.* Emma's heart lurched.

Nelson gave the signal for them to go up the stairs, to enter the hallway on the seventh floor.

"Wait here, Ramsey," Nelson whispered.

Emma nodded. *I wouldn't have gone with you if you asked me to.* She wished she believed it, wished she had the strength to defy an order.

Nelson led Patersall and Basada down the hall, listening at each door he passed, but didn't find what he was searching for. Finally, he approached the door at the end, listened, then nodded to the other men. Emma felt a cold dread wash over her.

"Nobody move!" Nelson shouted as Basada kicked the door down with a sickening crunch. Terrified screams. A young family.

Patersall marched into the room and grabbed a young girl by the hand, dragging her into the hall. "I've got you now!"

"You're all coming with us, whether you like it or not!" Basada shouted over their panicked cries.

As a scream of anger came from the bowels of the apartment, a doorway halfway between Emma and Nelson opened, and two figures emerged, pointing weapons at the men.

"Nobody's going anywhere," said a cold, firm voice—a slim man holding a revolver.

The other figure, a stocky man wearing a balaclava, aimed a crossbow at Basada.

Emma felt time slow down.

A woman burst through the doorway behind Corporal Nelson, long brown hair flowing behind her, a knife in her hands. "Let my Ivy go, you monsters!"

"Don't take another step!" Basada barked, as he raised his assault rifle and turned towards the woman. The mother.

Maybe she tried to stop. Maybe she was going so fast she couldn't.

A round of semi-automatic fire filled the hall, echoing through the building.

She dropped to her knees then collapsed, the knife clattering on the wooden floorboards.

Emma wanted to run, to get away from the

nightmare, but she couldn't move.

"Goddammit, Corrine!" The man in the balaclava fired.

Basada fell to the ground, a crossbow bolt lodged in his neck, blood spurting across the walls.

Patersall held the girl, beating at him with her tiny fists and screaming for her mother.

"Guns on the floor," the slim man shouted amidst the chaos, his shaking revolver aimed at Nelson. "We aren't going anywhere."

Her heart racing, Emma could only watch as Nelson smiled and pulled the trigger.

Nothing happened. His gun was jammed.

Patersall threw the child against a wall with a heavy thunk and reached for the assault rifle slung around his shoulder. He was too late. The reloaded crossbow was already aimed at his face.

"You touch that gun, you die," hissed the man with the crossbow.

Patersall froze, his face pale.

Nelson looked down the hall to where Emma stood, a smile on his face. "Private Ramsey, kill these fuckers!"

Crap. The blood in her veins turned to ice as the two men turned on her, anger gleaming in their eyes.

Fuck. Fuck. Fuck.

Emma stood there, frozen. Her assault rifle shook in her hands. She had to shoot. She had to protect Nelson and Patersall. *I can't shoot civilians.* She took a step backwards, towards the stairwell. "Corporal, no, sir!"

The man with the revolver smiled.

"Private Ramsey, that's an order!"

"Corporal, no." Emma raised her arms in the air, tears streaming down her face. This was going to cost her everything, but this was one order she could not obey.

The man with the revolver took a step towards her. "Weapons on the ground."

She fell to her knees, placing her gun on the floor.

Patersall bolted while everyone was watching her surrender. He darted into an empty room and disappeared.

The crossbow fired, sending a bolt after him.

Emma watched, a scream stuck in her throat, as Nelson smashed the stock of his M4 carbine into the face of the man in the balaclava.

As the man with the revolver turned back to the struggle, Emma tried to run for the stairs, but her knees were locked, frozen in fear.

The deafening sound of the revolver firing was the last thing she heard.

CHAPTER FIFTEEN

The sound of thunder woke David from his watery nightmares. Head throbbing, the stench of vomit making him gag, he staggered to his feet and looked out the window into the darkness.

Something wasn't right. That wasn't thunder. That was gunfire.

His heart skipped a beat. The flash flash flash of machine-gun fire reflected off the glass buildings. A black militia speedboat weaved through the choppy water, firing at the towers. A flare gun and a half-empty bottle of rum sat on the windowsill. *Oh no.*

His conversation with Elise and Alfred came

back to him through the murk. They'd given him a job as a lookout, to watch out for the militia's speedboats. They'd said it was too dangerous for him to go after Sal. If he couldn't go after his son, David at least wanted to be able to shoot the fuckers who took him. But they wouldn't listen. Full of anger and frustration he climbed the stairs to his post, bringing a bottle of rum with him for company.

More speedboats roared to life, filling the city with the sounds of their engines. *The sky should be red.* David's eyes fell to the flare gun on the windowsill. *My job.*

As he reached for the flare gun, a glowing ball of light shot up into the darkness and the sky exploded into crimson. Another lookout had fired a flare into the sky. *Too late. They were both far too late.*

Panicked, David could only watch, his heart racing, as the speedboats roared through the city and sped past his tower back to the mainland.

He staggered down a flight of stairs, instinctively going for the boat, wanting to try and help. He stopped on the next floor down, a moment of doubt, not knowing who needed help, or how to get there.

I should have been down there, waiting for those shitheads with a gun. His anger turned on himself. *I should have stayed awake. I should have done my fucking job.*

There was one thing he could do, the only thing within his power. His heart heavy, he staggered back up the stairs and finished the bottle.

Linda was waiting for him, her arms crossed, drops of water running down her legs, falling from her dress to the floor.

"You promised you'd never drink again." Her voice, a low hiss, was full of anger. "You've been given another chance, and what do you do? You screw it up."

"I'm sorry, I didn't mean—"

"Your people needed you, you prick. Salim needed you. *I needed you!*"

"I know, I know." He shook his head, tears streaming down his face.

"Don't fuck up again." Her voice softened. "Be strong. Be the father I always knew you would be."

CHAPTER SIXTEEN

Emma emerged from the sanctuary of sleep into painful consciousness. She lay on a mattress, her hands tied behind her back.

"You're awake," came a firm voice.

Emma nodded and twisted her body to the right, to look at the speaker. A woman sat in a leather recliner near the windows, thick red curtains blocking out the sunlight. Her eyes searched Emma's, her face stern, her short hair flecked with silver.

"Who are you, and don't give me that name rank and serial number bullshit."

"I'm Ramsey. Emma Ramsey." Her voice was

hoarse, her throat aching. She had nothing to hide. These people were going to kill her anyway, and there was nothing on the mainland worth protecting.

"Right. Emma, I'm Elise." Her voice was calm, conciliatory. "Can I get you anything? Water? Food?"

Emma shook her head.

"Okay, what happened last night?"

"They're dead, aren't they?" A cold stone of guilt lay in the pit of her stomach. *That woman. Basada. Who knows how many others?*

"Too many people died." Elise's voice trembled with anger. "And we came here to get away from all that violence and hatred."

A moment of silence. Emma closed her eyes, a shudder of grief and fear ripping through her. She wasn't able to save anyone. And now she was going to pay.

"All right, Emma. I've answered you. I just want you to answer my quest—" The door burst open and two men entered. One was stocky with red hair, a crossbow slung over his shoulder—the man who killed Basada. The other was a stranger, tall and full of anger.

The man with the crossbow looked at Elise. "Is she awake? Why didn't you tell us?"

The stranger pushed past Elise and stood over the bed. "You," he growled, staring at Emma with eyes full of hatred.

Her heart raced, she tried to twist away, but a heavy blow came down into her stomach, knocking the air out of her lungs.

"David, no!" shouted Elise, and she and the other man grabbed her attacker, pulling him back.

Emma struggled to breathe, her eyes blurring with tears. Anger and defiance ignited in her, and she twisted herself to glare at her captors, as Elise and the man who punched her disappeared outside, leaving behind the reek of alcohol and fear.

"What are we going to do with you?" The crossbow man's voice had lost the edge of hate it had carried last night. He paced back and forth, looking Emma up and down.

Emma avoided his gaze and stared at the ceiling. *I won't make this easy for you, you bastards.*

"You've been taking our people for months now," he said, his voice low and bitter. "Why can't you leave us alone?"

What could she say? *I was just following orders?* Still recoiling from the blow, her stomach in a knot of pain, she ignored him. She was their prisoner. But, if she stayed alive long enough, maybe she could find a way to escape.

And go where? Back to the ADF? She couldn't go

back.

She could go east—Messinger's influence only extended so far. *West?* No. Even if she went far enough west to escape Messinger, she'd end up in Adelaide—and that place was a nightmare even before the flood. East it was. If she could escape.

The door opened and Elise returned, her forehead creased in concern. "I'm sorry, Emma. Believe me, we wouldn't have let him in if we knew he was going to hit you."

"She's not talking, Elise."

"Give her time, Baker. She'll talk."

Fat chance, Emma thought. If she gave them the information they wanted, then they'd kill her—she knew it in her stomach.

Baker turned to the door. "I'm heading to Central. We need to plan for tonight."

"Get Todd up here—he's a nurse. I want to make sure she's not hurt."

Elise turned to Emma as the door closed. "I need answers. I need to keep my people safe."

Emma stared up at the ceiling. The eight downlights stared back at her, as useless as her attempts to rebuild the city.

"We're only trying to make a life for ourselves out

here. I might be a bitch, and David—the bloke who hit you—might be an arsehole at times, but we're not bad people. We didn't ask for this. To be harassed, to be attacked, to have friends and family disappear in the night." She paused, waiting for a reaction. Emma refused to give her one. Then, with her voice full of disgust, Elise said, "We don't usually take people prisoner. That's more your line of work, isn't it?"

Emma stared at the ceiling.

"Hell, most of our community are just trying to get away from people like *you*," Elise continued. "Trying get away from the beatings, the torment, the abuse. Just because they're different."

A knot of coiled resentment squirmed up into Emma's chest. "What's your goddamn point?" she hissed, finally making eye contact with Elise.

"I heard your corporal ordered you to shoot Hassan and Baker, but you refused. I've answered your questions. I just want you to answer mine. Why didn't you shoot?"

Because you're civilians! she wanted to shout, but she was caught between her anger at being taken prisoner, at being punched and interrogated, and her fear of these people—how could she trust them? They were armed, they shot Basada through the neck with a crossbow, fired at Patersall and Nelson as they tried to escape. Maybe they were as violent and dangerous as Messinger had always said.

"Emma, if there's a decent person somewhere underneath all that G.I. Jane bullshit, it's time for you to come out. What's left of the world needs to unfuck itself, and that starts with the people in it. We've all lost so much to the waves. We all want to rebuild."

Emma shut her eyes, guilt and agony tearing through her core.

"You think it over, Emma." Elise said before leaving the room and locking the door behind her.

She was alone. Her defiance, her anger all left, and she lay on the bed: defeated, exhausted, and terrified.

***

Emma's gaze turned to the door. She'd heard footsteps and low voices on the other side.

"We think she's okay," said Elise, opening the door. "Still, I'd rest easier if you had a look."

A slim man with a cropped red beard entered. A chill ran up Emma's spine. Familiar. *She knew this man.*

"Okay," his soft voice filled the room as he approached. "I'm Todd McCarthy. I'm a nurse—*was* a nurse—and I'm just going to check that you're in good shape."

Emma's heart raced as his eyes locked onto hers. *No!* A look of recognition. A look of disgust.

"Elise, could you give me a moment with the patient?" His voice had turned bitter, full of loathing, and his eyes didn't leave Emma's as he waited for the sound of the door.

Laying helpless, bound to the bed, her blood turned to ice.

"You," he growled. "We'd been mugged and assaulted. And then you pricks arrived and beat the shit out of us."

A bolt of guilt and paralysing fear surged through her. "I didn't," she whispered in protest. "I didn't touch you."

"You stood there and watched your buddies beat us up," Todd sneered. "You're as bad as they are."

He was right. She should have done something, said something. But how could she, against the ADF?

"Let's get this over with," he said, beginning his examination. "Elise said David punched you? Let's start there."

Emma tried to squirm away from his hands.

"I'm not going to hurt you. I may not like you,

but I'm a doctor. I'm ethical." He reached for her again. "Not like you." Despite the anger behind his eyes and the scorn in his voice, Todd's touch was gentle.

As he worked, touching the sensitive skin of her stomach and taking her pulse, her temperature, Emma remembered the fight. Remembered how she didn't say a word, didn't do a damned thing to help the people who needed her the most. Claire's voice came to her, soft, full of promise and hope. *Our people.*

CHAPTER SEVENTEEN

David's mind was a whirlpool of pain, alcohol, and anger as he entered the prisoner's room. *Her* room. He had recognised her right away, her shoulder-length sandy ponytail. She had taken his son away.

Overcome with anger, he punched her, defenceless and tiny as she was.

Even before they tackled him out of the room, he knew he'd done the wrong thing. Everything he did was the wrong damn thing.

"I get it, Dave." Elise crossed her arms in front of her chest, her back to the door. "You're angry. Everything's gone to hell and you want someone to blame."

Under her stare, he dropped his eyes to the pale carpet, stained by decades of visitors to this old hotel, the Radisson. "I saw her in the boat, taking people away. She probably took Sal too, goddammit."

"And if she did, will beating her bring him back?"

David took a breath. Two breaths. "No." He shook his head and looked out over the Flagstaff Gardens, where the tops of trees—skeletal hands devoid of leaves—poked above the waves.

"She's one woman. She's not responsible for all the crimes of the entire ADF." Her disappointment in him was clear.

Then it clicked. "You want her. To join us, I mean."

"I don't know. Maybe. I can't figure her out. She could have killed Hassan and Baker—she was ordered to shoot them—but she refused."

"She's the enemy. She took Sal—"

"The surest way to make someone think of you as their enemy is to treat them as your enemy." Elise's frustration was clear.

David put his head in his hands. *Maybe I really messed up.*

"And look, whatever else she may have done, she

didn't fire on us when she was ordered to. Maybe we can get through to her. Maybe she can help. You take a breather out here, okay?"

David fell into a waiting faux-leather couch. Elise headed towards the door.

"Wait, Elise. Tell her I'm sorry."

"Tell her yourself."

The door closed, leaving David alone with his pain, his confusion and his shame. *What would Linda think?* He asked himself. He had never been a violent man, an angry man. He'd never been so driven by emotion, by hate and fear before. Had the wave changed him so much? That profoundly?

There was no doubt the wave had changed the entire world. *Hell, it changed Linda into a fucking corpse. There's no bloody wonder if it's changed me too.*

***

That evening, David sat by the radio as the community gathered, shocked and scared. Corinne, Vashti and Sippo had been killed by the militia, shot by machine guns while they tried to protect themselves, to defend their families.

No-one had thought the Militia would do that. Sure, they were capable of violence and brutality, but no-one saw this coming. They hadn't stopped there, either. Stefan, Adrian, Raquel and Ingrid had been captured, with further reports of others missing as more people arrived at Central Island.

David balled his hands into fists, full of self-loathing and guilt. He didn't make eye-contact with anyone. He didn't look up when Baker stood next to him, his hand on David's shoulder.

"You okay, mate?"

David shrugged.

"Look, this isn't your fault, okay? We all knew they'd come back. Everyone knew to keep their lights out, to be on their guard. The extra warning the flares might have provided wouldn't have changed much."

David nodded. Baker was a good guy, trying to make him feel better. But David was too far into the nightmare to come out that easily.

"What are we going to do?" Martin asked, when everyone had assembled.

"We have to keep calm," said Alfred. "We have to keep our heads."

"I'm more worried about keeping my daughter safe." Baker's voice was fierce.

The conversation washed over David as he scanned the faces in the crowd and caught Kintha's eye.

Despite the pain and sadness beneath her dark curls, she gave him a small smile. *What must she think of me now?*

David was jolted out of his misery by an announcement on the radio.

"Citizens of Melbourne. Last night, our Defence Force personnel attempted an operation to recover and return—"

"Everyone, listen to this!" David turned the volume up. "Messinger's talking about last night."

"The criminals who reside in the towers attacked us, killing Lance-Corporal Basada and Private Jacobs, with Corporal Nelson and Privates Patersall and Sommers injured, and Private Ramsey MIA. These soldiers had been nothing but dedicated to rebuilding our community. These parasites, these terrorists will be brought to justice. I want to assure every one of you that they will not get away with this. By their actions, the people of the drowned city have shown that they are dangerous, that they are a threat to us all. It's only a matter of time before they start attacking us, and they won't think twice about killing any of us in our sleep."

"How dare they?" Murmurs of anger and resentment spread through the community.

"We have no choice but to take this extremely seriously. From this moment forward, anyone seen leaving the city will be arrested. Anyone suspected of communicating or supplying these criminals, these terrorists, will be apprehended and brought to justice. Anyone resisting arrest will be shot."

A stunned silence descended on the sea-borne community, punctuated only by the sloshing of the waves.

"That's a declaration of war." Alfred's thin voice was carried away on the breeze.

"We have to talk to them. This is insane," said Hassan, his voice grave.

"How?" asked Elise. "They won't listen."

"And if we try, we'll get arrested," Martin cut in. "Or shot. No bloody way."

Todd placed a hand on Martin's shoulder. "The militia almost beat me to death. And in their minds, those pricks let us off lightly. If we go back—if any of us go back—they won't be so nice."

"So what are we going to do?"

"It doesn't matter what we do. They're going to keep coming for us," said Alfred. "If we thought it was bad before, it'll be worse if we return with our tails between our legs."

Elise nodded, and murmurs of agreement spread through the group.

"I know we're concerned about our families," said Baker. "I'm scared to death about Freya's safety. But the new world Messinger's building—it's not for her."

"Okay." Alfred looked into the sea of faces. "We

need a plan for tonight. We've got to make sure no-one has their lights on, make it hard for them to know which buildings are inhabited, which are abandoned."

"The buildings that they've already found people in, they'll know some of us live there," said Elise. "There's a good chance they'll come back to those."

"The children, the elderly, those who don't want to fight. We'll need to guard them. Keep them safe," added Hassan.

"I'm not going to let them hurt my daughter," Baker said.

David sat through the meeting, listening to the plan for the city's defences, waiting to hear his name called. The lookouts had been announced, as well as the men and women who were to defend the city from the militia. His name had still not been mentioned.

As everybody left to take up their assigned positions, David approached Alfred and Elise.

"What can I do?"

They exchanged a glance.

"David, we know you were on the bottle last night when you were meant to be on lookout duty," said Alfred.

"We know it wasn't just you who didn't see the militia's boats until it was too late, so we aren't blaming you for last night's disaster . . ." Elise added.

"But so much has happened—you haven't had time to deal with Rafi, with Salim . . ."

"We think it would be best if you sat this one out, Dave. You need a break."

"No, that's bullshit," he protested. "Everyone's hurting, everyone's fraying at the edges. Everyone needs a break."

"Look, you're not wrong." Alfred's slow nod showed his weariness.

"And I need to do something. If I'm alone, I won't be able to sleep. I'll just turn back to the bottle. Please."

"Well, there is one thing," Elise said, her voice hesitant.

"What? I'll do anything."

"We haven't figured out how to deal with our prisoner."

"Elise, no!" hissed Alfred. "You know what he did to her."

"I'll guard her," David cut in. "I still need to apologise. I owe it to her."

"If you hurt her again, you're not going to be welcome amongst us anymore, David," Alfred warned.

"You don't need to worry about that," David

promised. "You believe me, don't you, Elise?"

She nodded, her eyes cold and hard.

Don't fuck this up.

CHAPTER EIGHTEEN

Emma lay on the bed like a starfish. Her arms and legs were tied to the bedposts, a blindfold over her eyes, a rag in her mouth. She'd been there for hours struggling at her restraints, anger and hopelessness building inside her.

Footsteps outside the door. She froze, her heart thumping. The door creaked open and someone entered the room. Elise? The bastard who punched her? There was no way to be sure.

"Emma?" A deep, masculine voice. A voice she knew.

Crap.

"Emma, listen—I'm sorry for hitting you."

Yeah, right.

"I wanted to get back at you, I wanted to hurt those who hurt me." His voice caught, on the verge of breaking. "But I shouldn't have punched you. That was wrong, and I apologise for that."

If I had ten bucks for every bullshit apology I've ever got, I'd be a goddamn millionaire. She felt the mattress shift as he sat down.

"I'm a salvager. I've been scuba diving—spending as much time in the sea as I could—ever since I was a teenager. And I've learned that monsters exist, they do. But not in the sea." He sighed, a broken sound.

There was something about this man—the way he carried his pain—that reached Emma. Despite her fear, despite the traces of his violence in the bruises on her body, despite flinching at his every word—she couldn't ignore his pain. *God, I'm pathetic.*

"When I saw you, my hatred took over. I could feel myself turning into a monster. I'm sorry." He whispered. "I'm sorry. I don't expect you to forgive me."

Emma waited, unable to speak even if she'd wanted to because of the rag in her mouth. Disgust mixed with compassion churned inside her.

"I'm not a violent man," he continued, anguish in his voice. "Or at least, I wasn't. And I don't want to be.

But that goddamn wave. My wife. And then my son. Everything's gone. Everything's changed, fucked up and ruined."

She held her breath as David stood up and paced the room.

"I can't stay here anymore." His voice was a harsh whisper. "This city is no place for monsters."

***

A silent eternity passed. Only Emma's muffled breaths filled the room.

She heard footsteps on the other side of the door, soft voices . . . but nobody entered.

David was pacing the room, pausing now and then near the wall with the window. Tension radiated from him, the stench of sweat, of fear.

What was he doing here?

The curtains rustled, and Emma imagined him looking out the window. "It's begun," he murmured. "They're here."

Emma wanted to ask what he'd seen, but she already knew. It could only be the army, her comrades on their way to rescue her. The idea should have pleased her, but it didn't. *My comrades? Corporal Nelson, Private Patersall?*

No goddamn way.

"Don't make a noise." David's hushed voice broke the silence.

What would happen if they heard me? If I screamed through my rag? Do I want to be rescued?

She lay there, helpless and frightened, as the sound of heavy boots echoed up the stairs.

"We better not be searching this hotel for nothing," hissed a familiar voice outside the door.

"I swear I saw faces upstairs, Corporal. The room with the open window."

Emma held her breath. A soft thump came from the floor above. *Oh no.* Her heart dropped to the floor.

"One more flight it is, then."

Tension filled the air as the sound of boots echoed up the stairs. David cursed under his breath.

Emma's heart raced, counting down the seconds until disaster.

Crash—a door was kicked open and shouts came from above.

Crack. A single gunshot echoed through the building.

The ceiling shook with the deafening *crack-crack-crack* of machine gun fire. Her heart tore apart as the gunfire ceased, leaving only a keening wail, high and desolate, in the air. *Oh, God.*

Boots stomped down the stairs, laughter echoed through the halls, hollow and empty.

The bed creaked underneath her as David sat down. Emma jerked away as his hand brushed against her cheek. He pulled off her blindfold, but she kept her eyes closed, her chest heaving in sobs, her heart full of despair.

Is he going to take his anger out on me again? Emma opened her eyes and looked up, her vision blurry with tears. She could make out his shape in the dark, hunched and defeated, his hand tensing in anger.

Her blood turned to ice. In David's hand was a sleek black pistol. After a tense moment, he made a move to get up and go after the soldiers, to exact revenge. *No— no more death.* Emma moved her arm as much as she could, brushed it against his to draw his attention.

The violence in him terrified her, but he was in pain. She knew that all too well. Emma looked up at him and shook her head, pleading with him not to go. He pulled the rag out of her mouth.

"Don't go," she whispered, her voice bruised.

"Why should I listen to you?" he hissed, venom in his voice.

"I don't want you to die. I don't want anyone else to die."

David nodded. Too many people were already dead. At least he could see that. "I'm going upstairs," he said, his voice curt.

"Take me with you." Her choked voice was a plea. "I want to help."

***

Emma's heart raced as David opened the door to the hallway. Footsteps could still be heard below, getting further and further away. His grip on her arm was vice-like, warning her against calling out for help. He didn't have to worry, speaking to those bastards was the last thing she wanted to do. They climbed the stairs together, his strong hand still gripping her arm, reminding her that she was his prisoner.

They reached the corridor on the upper floor.

"David . . ." A whisper from behind them. A figure lay on the ground, holding a revolver in his trembling hands.

David released Emma's arm, then staggered down the hallway to kneel by the figure.

"Hassan, it's okay," David said, his voice barely a whisper. "It's okay."

"I tried to stop them. I . . ." The weak voice

faltered and coughed, soft and wet.

"It's okay." David shook with grief, his face hidden behind his arm. "It's okay."

Emma turned away from David and took a step towards an open doorway. Pale moonlight fell on the bloodshed. Dark figures lay on the ground in pools of blood, seeping into the carpet. The acrid scent of gunfire filled the air, and she could almost taste the metallic tang of blood. Tiny, whimpering moans—people still clung to life.

David climbed to his feet and joined her, surveying the massacre. Emma's body tensed, shaking in despair. *How could they do this?*

Without a word David crept towards the nearest figure.

Emma was caught—she could run, she could escape. Yet she stood still, her heart breaking as she watched David brush the hair out of an elderly woman's eyes. Her thin fingers clutched his as she took deep ragged breaths. Her hands shook in spasms of fear and pain, then grew weaker and weaker.

Emma had to do something, but she was helpless in the face of all this need. She stepped into the room, drawn to a weak cry. A figure sat against the wall, a dark stain spreading across her pale jumper. Her eyes met

Emma's. The carpet beneath her feet was wet and dark and sticky with blood as she left her old life behind.

There was nothing either of them could do but sit with the mortally wounded until they passed, until they drew their last gasping, painful, heart-rending breath. Even if they had a medkit, a whole surgical team, they wouldn't have been able to save anyone.

In silence, they covered the bodies of the dead with blankets and bedsheets. With every innocent soul lost to the bloodshed, Emma's heart broke again. When she opened her mouth to speak, only a weak, wretched sob came out.

The rising sun of the new day found her and David huddled together, their clothes stained with blood, faces etched with mirrored grief and despair.

CHAPTER NINETEEN

The clouds hung heavy over Central Island as David sat amongst the community, exhausted and covered in blood. Emma, overwhelmed and alone, sat to his right. Kintha was next to David, her arms around his shoulders, tears in her red-rimmed eyes.

As seagulls dove into the water, images of last night's nightmare resurfaced in David's mind. All that blood. All that death. He'd released Emma as a prisoner, wondering if he was making a mistake. But she hadn't left. She hadn't tried to run. Instead, she chose to help the dying, to help him—even after he'd hit her. His gut twisted with nausea and disgust as he remembered that punch. Now they both wore the same uniform of blood and grief.

Alfred listed the names of the dead, each accompanied by a gull's plaintive cry. Every name brought a face to David's mind, an image of someone ripped apart by bullets, bleeding out on the floor. Emma flinched with each name. She hadn't known any of them in life, but she knew too many of them in death, in their final agonising moments.

After the names were read, a moment of silence passed.

Then another.

People looked towards Alfred and Elise, waiting for something. Hope? An answer?

Elise stepped forward and scanned the crowd, her eyes meeting David's. Then they focused on Emma. A moment of panic—was Elise going to blame her? Call her out? But no, something passed between them. Elise nodded, and her stern look softened.

After glancing up into the dark cloudy skies, Elise turned back to the group. "There's no way around it, folks. We're at war. They're going to come back, again and again."

"What do they want, though? Why do they hate us?" Kintha asked.

"They want to take us back to the mainland, force us to rebuild the city. Messinger blames us for Jagannatha, remember?"

"Idiot," Freya growled.

"This is our city," said Elise. "They aren't going to stop, but we can't give up. This is our home. We must fight back, defend our families. What we tried last night—hiding our most vulnerable members—didn't work. We need a new plan."

Murmurs of agreement rippled through the group.

"No-one has to stay," Alfred said. "You can return to the mainland, but you know what kind of reception Messinger has waiting for you. If you try to go around the coast, they'll watch. They'll send their speedboats after you, and if you're rowing, if you're sailing, you won't be fast enough."

"I want to stay," said Baker. "But we're not fighters. We're just people. Broken, lost, afraid."

"No," Kintha said. "We're not lost. We're home. We're together."

Emma stirred next to David. "Where we're needed," she muttered through her pain and confusion.

"We know this city," Elise said. "We know these towers. We've got to use that to our advantage."

Throughout the group, people nodded, indicating their agreement.

"We all need to make some tough decisions. Alfred and I will think of new tactics, anyone who wants to help is welcome. Everyone else, rest up and we'll meet up this evening."

The meeting was over, with a hopeless sense that their peaceful community had been dealt a fatal blow.

Elise approached David, Emma and Kintha.

"David, Emma, you need rest. You both need to clean up," Elise said. "We can take you back to the Radisson."

Emma flinched. "I don't want to go back there."

"Fair enough," said Elise. "Look, what you did back there . . . It's obvious that you're different from the other soldiers. That you have a heart. If you want to stay with us, we can set you up in an apartment in the QV towers."

"Or you can both come to mine to get cleaned up. I'm Kintha, by the way. A fisher, and a friend of Dave and Sal's."

David felt like he'd been punched. *Sal.*

"Sorry," Kintha said, seeing his reaction. "I wasn't sure if you were ready to go back to your place . . ."

"I'll go with you, Kintha," Emma said. "I need to get clean."

"I'll take you back to yours then, Dave?" Elise asked.

David nodded. He didn't have the strength to go back alone.

CHAPTER TWENTY

Emma sat in a rowboat as Kintha fought the waves, taking them to her home. She was still in shock from last night's bloodshed and needed time to recover, time to think. More than anything, she wanted to be able to get clean, safe from David's violence and Elise's intense gaze.

"My place isn't much and it stinks of fish, I hope that's okay," Kintha said. "I can lend you some clothes, though they probably smell as well." She smiled, and Emma couldn't help but smile too.

Kintha rowed the boat through a smashed window in the side of a building and tied it up to a bench. The stench of dead fish filled the room, and Emma gagged.

"I told you," Kintha said with a laugh.

Emma nodded, grimacing as she looked down at her blood-stained uniform. "It still smells better than I probably do."

"Follow me." Kintha got out of the boat. "It's better upstairs."

Emma followed Kintha, looking around at the apartment. "This is nice. I live in an empty steel hangar." She thought for a moment. "Lived."

"Come on, the shower's through there."

"You have running water?" Emma asked, surprised.

"No, just a gravity shower. A bucket filled with fresh water with holes in the bottom."

"Where do you get the fresh water from?"

"David. He's rigged up basic desal systems for most of the community."

Emma nodded, impressed with the tenacity of the people she always imagined lived in slums.

∗∗∗

After scrubbing the grime and blood from her skin, Emma dried off with a towel. She had wanted to spend longer in the shower, longer alone, but didn't want to use all of Kintha's water. She felt refreshed, but doubted she'd ever feel truly clean again. Kintha had laid out some clothes: jeans and a simple grey shirt. They fit okay, and only slightly stank of fish. Now she needed answers, and Kintha was waiting for her.

"How was the shower?"

"It was good, and thanks for the clothes."

"Happy to help."

"But why are you helping me?" Emma crossed the room and sat down at a table.

"Why wouldn't I?"

"I'm your enemy. I've taken your friends back to the mainland. And just last night my . . ." She faltered, unable to say the words.

Kintha smiled. "That's why. You don't think of yourself as one of them. You had the chance to leave, but you stayed."

Emma shuddered, recalling the blood, the horror of last night.

"And I heard you at the meeting. You said we are 'where we're needed.' I don't know what you meant, exactly, but I have an idea."

Emma nodded. "Thanks for everything, for being so nice."

"That's all good, Emma. Now I bet you're exhausted. You can rest up here if you like."

She wanted nothing more than to lay down and block out her nightmares for a few hours. Emma felt safe in Kintha's company, safer than she had in weeks. But she shook her head. Now that she was refreshed and had a chance to clear her head, she knew she needed to go to David. Despite his violence, he was a broken man. They had both been shattered by last night, they were both wrought with grief and guilt. He was the only one who understood her heartache and pain, and he had already shown he trusted her. "Take me to David."

***

Emma sat in an office chair, hands around a mug of black coffee. Across the table sat David, looking around the office as if he was the stranger here. Last night, as they had sat with the dead and the dying, an unspoken, if uneasy bond had developed between them. Not friendship. Emma still felt the blow of his fist to her stomach when she saw his hands. But a kinship of sorts. She could not have endured the utter devastation without him. They sat in silence, both wanting to say something, both wanting the other to go first.

Emma looked around the office. Rows of tables adorned with useless computer monitors and telephone headsets. "This was the Origin Energy call centre, wasn't it? I knew someone who worked here, before. . ."

David nodded. "Before Jagannatha. Before the wave changed everything. Killed everything." He laughed weakly, tinged with bitterness and regret. "Maybe it would have been better if it did."

"How did you survive the wave?"

David shuddered and shook his head.

"Sorry. Let's talk about something else."

"Emma, I'm sorry I hit you . . . I can't believe I did that." He looked down at his trembling hands. "I'm not that guy," he whispered as he clenched his hand into a fist, then opened it.

She shifted in her seat, unable to hide her unease.

"Why'd you join the Mainland Militia?" he asked, his soft voice hostile and guarded.

The answer was simple. "I joined them because I wanted to help."

"And do you think you lot have helped?" he challenged, his eyes flashing in anger. "Does persecuting people out of the fear of another asteroid help? Is abducting our kids helping, dammit?"

"No." Her stomach clenched, weathering his

brief, predictable storm. "It's a nightmare, what they have us do."

"Why didn't you leave?"

"Because I'm a coward." She looked him in the eye, then down to her coffee. "Because that uniform, that gun protected me from being beaten, from being raped . . ."

David nodded, rubbing his stubble. "Why didn't you run off last night when you had the chance?"

"Where could I have gone?" Emma sighed. "Elise spoke to me earlier that day. She said 'what's left of the world needs to unfuck itself, and that includes the people in it.' That if there's a decent person underneath all my G.I. Jane bullshit it's time for her to come out. And she's right." An anxious dread wormed through her chest.

David watched her from across the table, waiting.

"It's time for me to come out," Emma whispered, closing her eyes. "It's time to stop living in fear. It's time to stop being such a damn coward." She felt the blood pump through her veins, felt a chain around her chest rattle loose. She breathed in, breathed out, opening her eyes. "It's time for me to come out," Emma repeated, stronger, her voice full of fear and hope. "So here I am."

David nodded from across the table. "I'm glad

you're here. That you didn't go back . . ."

"I couldn't. Not anymore." She hesitated, her voice quavering. *Did he get it? Did he understand?* "David, if I went back, they'd arrest me, put me in the labour camps. I'm one of those people that they blame for Jagannatha. I . . ." Her body shook, her hands clenching against her clothes. "I like men. And women, too. I'm bisexual. And I'm not going to hide it from anyone anymore."

An awkward silence hung between them.

"Th-thank you for trusting me." David's eyes were warm, compassionate. "You're safe here, well as safe as you can be." He shrugged. "That's a big deal. Are you okay? Is there anything—?"

Emma shook her head, picked up her coffee and lay back in the chair. She didn't have to hide who she was anymore. It felt good. Weird. Empowering. When you've got nothing left, you only have yourself.

CHAPTER TWENTY-ONE

David took the empty coffee cups to the kitchen and came back with two bottles of water. Emma still sat in the office chair, a woman transformed.

"Elise is a smart one," he said, wanting to fill the silence. "Maybe she's not the nicest, but she's smart. But then, who am I to talk?"

Emma watched in silence as he returned to the table.

"You mentioned nightmares. My nightmares have all come true. Linda and I came into the city, a romantic weekend getaway for our anniversary. We were in a hotel not far from here. A nice one. We'd been relaxing in the spa, our music drowning out the sound of the alarms. We didn't hear the warnings to evacuate until it was too late, but . . ." He gestured towards the mainland.

"Even if you did, you wouldn't have escaped the wave."

"Our room wasn't high enough. The door burst off its hinges, pinning Linda down as the room flooded. It was chaos. The water swept me away, but she was stuck. I tried to fight the wave, to get the door off her, but I couldn't. I tried . . ." The fear in Linda's eyes, her voice screaming his name returned to him. Grief constricted his heart. *I should have tried harder.* "We'd been trying for a baby for years. It was all she wanted, to be a mum. I wanted it for her. But I didn't think I was ready to be a dad."

Emma looked across at him, sympathy in her grey eyes.

"After the flood, after I had lost my wife—lost everything, I met a terrified kid picking through the ruins. He was an orphan of the waves. He'd seen both his parents drown. We looked after each other, we each filled the void that our family had left."

"Where is he?" Emma's voice was strained, like she already knew the answer.

"You took him." David said, his voice soft. "He's probably starving in one of your labour camps right now."

She turned to him, bold yet apprehensive. "He's about fourteen, dark skin, wearing a green hoodie?"

The blood froze in his veins. *That was him. That was Salim.* He nodded, not taking his eyes from her.

"He's not in a labour camp."

"How do you know?"

"At least, I don't think he is. I let him escape."

"You what? Where is he?"

"I don't know. He jumped out of the boat and ran right for the barracks. I caught up to him. I told him to go east. Get away from the city, follow the coast, get somewhere safe."

"Shit." David couldn't believe it. Sal was still out there. He believed her when she said Sal had run. That's just what he would have done. He had to go after him. He had to go after his son.

"We need to go to Central."

***

Together, David and Emma launched the boat into the deep. The afternoon sun shone down on them, reflecting off the silver and blue towers. Figures scurried to and fro between the buildings, calling out to them as they passed. They docked at Central, sending a wing of gulls into the air, and were greeted by Alfred and Elise.

"I heard you were on your way." Elise leant forward to offer her hand.

"Thanks." David looked into her troubled eyes and stepped onto the island.

"How are you holding up, Emma?" Alfred asked, helping Emma out of the boat.

"I've seen better days."

"I don't doubt that," Elise answered, looking at them with something approaching warmth. "You guys have to rest."

David grunted. "No time."

"What's this about?"

"Sal's not in the labour camps. He's free, heading east."

"I'm guessing you told him that?" Alfred turned to Emma, mistrust in his voice.

"Yes," Emma said, unflinching. "I was in the squad that took him back to the mainland. When we landed, he bolted."

"Go on."

"I caught up to him. But I didn't want to bring

him in. He was just a kid." She shrugged. "That's not who I am."

"Still, how can we trust you?" Alfred asked.

"I believe her," David said. "She's one of us now."

Elise searched Emma's face.

"I've come out," Emma whispered, vulnerable, but full of hope. "I'd wanted to leave the army for weeks, but I was scared. I was safe there—or I thought I was—as long as I kept my secret. But the things they've done. The things I've done. I need to make amends. That starts with reuniting the families I tore apart."

"Elise, Alf, I don't want to abandon you," David said. "But I have to go after Sal. If there's any chance he's alive and free . . ."

"I understand. When would you want to go?"

"Tonight."

Alfred sighed. "We won't try to stop you, though you'll be missed."

"What's your plan?" Elise asked.

"Well, that depends." David turned to Emma. "What kind of defences are there along the coast? How far does Messinger's territory extend?"

Emma turned her gaze towards the mainland. "There's barbed wire walls and patrols all along from

Tarneit to Clayton. Lookouts at Essendon Fields, St Albans and Box Hill."

"What about further south?" Alfred asked. "Aren't there islands down where Frankston used to be?"

Emma nodded. "That's right. If we head south while their attention is on the city, if we can get a boat fast enough, we can make a break for it. We can make it to those islands and head further east, to Warragul, the next day."

Elise turned to David. "But how will you find Sal?"

"I don't know, but I've got to try."

CHAPTER TWENTY-TWO

Watching the community work together, Emma felt a pang of regret. She could see why these people didn't want to leave the drowned city, why they fought to keep what they had.

"Emma, are you okay?" Elise asked.

"I'm okay. Kinda sad to be leaving here so soon." Emma looked over at the towers.

"You can always come back." Elise smiled at Emma with something approaching hope in her eyes.

Emma nodded and looked down. "I'm not sure I'd ever feel accepted here." The boatloads of people she'd taken from the towers haunted her, their terrified, hopeless faces. "But I want to help. I want David and Sal to have friends here to come back to."

Elise nodded. "That's what I want, too. I want to protect our people."

"I think I can help you with your defences," said Emma. "Before I leave."

"How can we improve?"

"You're too reactive. You hide in the shadows, only fighting back once you've been found. And by then, you've lost your main advantage."

"What advantages do we have?"

"Two key advantages. They're coming to you. They target buildings where they see light, see movement, so confuse them. Set candles burning in empty buildings. Set traps. But your major advantage is they're coming to you over water. Hit them when they're in their boats, in the open, vulnerable. Once they get inside, you lose that advantage. Unless you're setting a trap for them, don't let them land."

Elise nodded. "Thanks, Emma. That gives me hope."

***

Emma watched David farewell his friends. She had only

been with these people for a couple of days, but seeing how they looked after each other, Emma had new hope about what survivors all over Australia could accomplish.

One by one, the members of the community came forward to say goodbye. Each of them embraced David and didn't even look at her. Not even the nurse, who she sought out with her eyes, an apology on her lips. *What difference would it make?*

Kintha approached with a teenage girl in tow. "Emma, this is Freya."

"We all love David, and we love Sal," Freya said, a quaver in her voice. "He trusts you, so we do too. Look after him."

Kintha stepped forward and hugged Emma, holding her tight. "Please look after Dave for me," she whispered. "And if you can, bring him back. Bring them both back."

Emma hugged her back. "Thank you, Kintha. I'll do what I can."

***

Dressed in wetsuits, half submerged amongst the ruins, Emma and David waited for the speedboats. She held David's black pistol, cold and heavy in her hands. Emma hoped Salim had listened to her, had headed east. If he hadn't—if he'd been caught by another patrol or if he'd stayed in the city—this might all be for nothing. They had to find Sal—for his sake, for David's, and for her own. There were so many families she had helped divide, so many things she had to atone for. It all started with reuniting David with his adopted son.

Candles had been lit halfway up the sandy brown ANZ tower on Collins Street. Through its large windows, the light drew the soldiers like moths. As Emma and David waited in the cold water, two speedboats arrived and circumnavigated the building. The boats docked right in front of them, and Emma held her breath as the soldiers climbed through a window. She could see little more than black shapes against the building. The moon was behind thick clouds, threatening rain.

Tense minutes ticked by. In the darkness where the boats had docked, a flash of orange lit up a pale, gaunt face. Fulham's face. After the flame winked out, a pinpoint of red light remained. Emma felt David's elbow against her ribs, nodding towards the soldier. This was the moment she had dreaded. They needed to take a speedboat, and this was the only way. She trained the sights on the glowing tip of his cigarette, following as it moved up and across, then glowed momentarily brighter.

Holding her breath, feeling the blood pump through her skull, she squeezed the trigger. The crack of the gunshot echoed through the city as the bright glow vanished.

Without hesitation, David swam towards the boat through the frigid water, one hand holding a backpack above the waves. Her hands trembling, Emma flicked the safety on the pistol and tucked it into her wetsuit, fumbling with the zip. *I just killed someone.*

"Come on!" David hissed, looking back at her.

Emma took a breath and pushed off towards the boats, praying they wouldn't be spotted. She forced her legs and arms into action and reached the boats first.

There was a faint gurgling, gasping sound. *He was still alive.*

Emma swam to the pale concrete wall of the building and pulled herself out of the water. Fulham looked up at her, his mouth a mess of blood, teeth, and shattered bone. He was drowning in his own blood. Her stomach twisted in revulsion and guilt as he shuddered, as the sickening gurgling faded to nothing.

David went straight to Fulham's body and stripped him of his assault rifle before jumping into the other speedboat. They worked in silence, only the beating of their hearts, the sloshing of the waves and the distant clap of thunder echoed through the city. Emma started up the boat while David cut the tethers. With a jerk they were free, and the sound of their stolen speedboat cut through the night.

Emma steered the boat south down Collins Street, pushing through the choppy water above a ritzy shopping strip, then turned right as they passed the dark blue glass wall of a Collins St tower. Her heart sank as the engines of other speedboats echoed through the city. *That was fast.*

"Turn left!" David hollered from the stern. "We've got to go south."

Emma swung the speedboat to the left, down a wide street lined with pale ruins.

"Shit, they're behind us. Head to Eureka!"

Emma nodded, her loose hair whipping back behind her. She would turn, but not yet. A pale concrete tower emerged in the distance. *There.*

A crack of gunfire behind them.

"Turn!" David's panicked voice came from the back of the boat.

"When I say 'now', get to the port side of the boat!" She hoped he'd heard her over the engines and the thunder. She cut back the throttle as they approached the pale building and shouted "Now!" She swung the boat to the left—so sharply she could have reached out and touched the water. Her heart lurched as the speedboat hurtled around the corner. They were going too fast— they were going to crash!

Ahead of them loomed two dark towers, a wall of dark glass and a wall of concrete. Between them was the slightest gap. She straightened the boat, pushing it forward towards the gap—no more than a couple of metres wide—her heart thumping in her chest.

"We won't make it!" David shouted from the stern, panic clear in his voice.

Emma agreed, but they were going too fast to stop, to change course. *This was going to be tight.* Fighting the urge to close her eyes, she aimed the bow of the speedboat between the buildings. They flashed through the gap as the glass panels above them exploded in a barrage of gunfire.

"Shit!" David shouted. "Where'd you learn to drive this thing?"

Emma smiled, adrenaline pushing her on as the Southbank towers appeared ahead of them, nothing now but glistening monuments of humanity's failure.

CHAPTER TWENTY-THREE

David crouched in the stern with the dead soldier's machine gun in the crook of his arm. In pursuit—barely visible against the darkness—were two black ADF speedboats, hell-bent on capturing or killing them.

"Fire at the bastards!" Emma shouted as another round of gunfire shot above their heads.

He looked back at her, crouched low behind the helm, pale hair streaming out behind her in the moonlight. Getting closer and closer every second was the Eureka tower, a thin pillar of blackness against the night sky. He hoped they'd get there in time.

The weapon felt heavy in his hands. Cold and

lethal. In the tower ahead, two figures leant out of a smashed window, illuminated by the soft glow of Christmas lights. Baker and Alfred. *Thank Christ.*

There was a flash of light and an ear-splitting *crack* as Alfred fired his rifle at the pursuing speedboats.

David turned back. The boats were still there.

Another crack from the heavens illuminated a soldier as he flew over the edge of a speedboat, crossbow bolt through his chest.

"He got one!" shouted David, ecstatic. "Thank you, Baker!"

A round of machine gun fire responded. The sound of glass shattering. They sped past Eureka tower and Emma swung the boat to the right, putting a wall of steel and glass between them and the pursuing speedboat then she swerved between the ruins of the casino complex.

"When you get a shot, take the bastards out!" Emma shouted.

Trying not to think about his friends, David turned his attention back to the machine gun. It seemed easy enough—point and shoot. He'd get them this time. He had to. *For Baker.* Heart racing, he waited for their pursuers to come back into sight between the buildings.

There! He held his breath and pulled the trigger.

Nothing.

"It's stuck, I can't shoot!" *Maybe the safety was on? Did guns like this even have safety switches?* His hands trembling, he tried to find the safety, but couldn't. *Dammit.* "It's no good, Emma. I can't get it to fire. We'll have to switch."

Leaving the weapon in the stern, David staggered forward, bracing himself as the boat burst through a wave.

Emma looked up, her eyes locked onto his. "Keep her steady, David."

"I've got it." His hand grabbed the wheel, just above hers.

A crack of thunder split the heavens. No—it wasn't thunder, it was Alfred's rifle. Gripping the wheel, David pushed the speedboat through another wave as Emma made her way to the stern.

He looked back to see her crouched down, hair whipping around her face, machine gun at the ready.

A shadow burst through the wave behind them, the spray of water caught in the moonlight. Emma squeezed the trigger and a burst of fire, thunderous and fatal, headed towards their pursuers.

"Missed!" The frustration was clear in her voice.

A thin ruin loomed ahead of them, a lone pale

figure of twisted steel. It was so easy to forget a thriving community used to live below them.

Another round of gunfire as they sped past. David shivered at the helm and pushed the speedboat harder, wanting to lose them amongst the waves, amongst the night.

"Cut speed, give me a better shot at them!"

David obeyed, then turned to see Emma standing up, bracing her foot on the edge of the boat. She was looking down the sights of the machine gun, waiting for them to burst through a wave. As she fired, the boat was rocked by another wave. David's heart lurched as Emma stumbled, falling backwards into the boat and landing with a heavy thunk.

"Are you okay?" David shouted. He glanced forward—nothing ahead but the empty ocean. He left the helm, took a step to where Emma lay.

"I'm okay." She turned to him, her expression fierce. "I told you to keep the bloody boat steady."

"Sorry," he said, as a burst of machine gun fire hit the boat. His leg exploded in burning agony. *Shit.*

"We've been hit!"

"No shit." He gasped through the pain. "My leg . . ."

"Fuck." Emma scrambled to her knees and

explored his leg through the wetsuit. "It's okay, the bullet's gone through. You'll be okay, I think."

"What are we going to do?"

Emma reached underneath a seat, pulled out a medkit and wrapped a bandage around his leg. "Hopefully this will stop the bleeding."

David grunted in pain as she pulled the bandage tight.

"You stay in the back." She pulled open the neck of her wetsuit and pulled out the pistol. "Use this or the F88, just give the bastards hell. I'll get us out of here."

David slid through the blood and water into the stern, the warm pistol shaking in his hands, his leg aching. *Damn.* He scanned the waves. *I'll give those shitheads hell, don't you worry.*

The boat lurched forward, weaving through the waves. *There!* Seeing the pursuing speedboat, David aimed and fired. *Crack!*

Moments passed, and the pursuing boat didn't reappear. With every second, more water filled the boat through the bullet holes in the deck.

"It's getting wet back here!"

"Give me a minute. Are they still behind us?"

"I can't see them."

"Start bailing out the water. There should be a

bucket back there."

Not taking his eyes off the horizon, David dragged the bucket through the water and tipped it over the side. Bucket after bucket, and still no sight of their pursuers.

"I can't see them anymore, I think we lost them."

They scanned the waves, looking for their enemy.

"Do you know where we are? How far south we've gone?" David panted. No matter how much he bailed out, the water kept getting deeper and deeper.

"Not far enough. Frankston's forty kilometres south of the city, we can't have gone half that."

Damn. "We won't make it to Frankston."

"I know. But I'm sure we've made it past the Box Hill lookout, now we need to get past Clayton."

"You're serious? You're taking us back into Messinger's territory?"

"You said it yourself, we won't make it to Frankston. We're out of options."

David glanced behind them. Still no sign of pursuit. "At least we've lost them."

"You really think we'd be that lucky?" Emma grunted.

"No." A quick smile crossed his face before he turned back to the bucket. "No way in hell." The water in the boat was dark with his blood. Unless he kept bailing it out they'd sink before they reached land.

Pain shot up his leg and David gasped as he tipped another bucket of water over the side.

"You're struggling. We should switch."

David nodded and limped to the helm. "What will the world be like when the sun comes up?" he asked, looking for any sign of land.

"Still fucked." Emma's eyes met his and she smiled. "But maybe with a bit more hope than before."

***

A wave crashed against something in the distance, the white spray catching the faint moonlight. A building.

"Emma—look." David shouted, pointing to the left. Together they watched as more and more buildings emerged from the sea. "We should cut the engine," he panted through the pain. "Row from here."

Emma pulled out the oars from beneath the seats as David cut the engine. Together they rowed, battling the waves, navigating around ruined buildings, the only sounds the crash of the waves and the cry of gulls.

A mountain emerged from the sea, covered in the trunks of pale dead trees.

"Let's get into those trees, find shelter," David said.

Emma nodded, casting another look behind her. They hadn't seen another boat for a while, but she still felt uneasy. As they approached the mountain she jumped into the water and dragged the boat to land.

David passed Emma the machine gun and backpack. As he set foot on land, agony shot through his leg. Gasping in pain, he fell forward onto the cold earth.

Together they stumbled up the hill, weak, exhausted, and cold to the bone.

"I can't go much further," he gasped, bolts of pain shooting up his leg every time he set his foot down.

"Up there, look." Emma pointed into the darkness.

"What is it?"

"A boat." They stumbled, breathless, to where the pale shape of a half disintegrated wooden rowboat stuck out amongst the trees.

David thumped what was left of the upside down boat. Nothing. "This will have to do." He leant against the wreckage and tore off his wetsuit before pulling out some dry clothes from the backpack.

"Let me have a look at that leg."

David complied, and Emma wiped the blood

away. "It's gone clean through." That was good news. "You've lost a lot of blood. Have some water, I'll clean it up."

"When we find Sal, would you want to go back to the city?" David asked, trying to distract himself from the pain.

"Let's just focus on finding Sal first."

"Good idea."

Emma finished re-wrapping the bandage around David's shin. "I'd feel better if we could take you to a hospital."

"Be a lot easier if they weren't all run by the militia." David grimaced.

"True." Emma nodded, a thoughtful expression on her face. "You sleep. I'll take first watch."

David was too tired to argue.

CHAPTER TWENTY-FOUR

Emma shivered against the hull of the rowboat, watching for any movement between them and the waterline. Cold and exhausted, she fought the urge to nestle against David's body, to share some of his warmth. She was still nauseated by his touch, she still couldn't forgive his violence, but a bond had formed between them, born from a shared nightmare of blood and pain.

Over the last few days the foundations of her world had shifted. Again. After what she'd seen, she could never return to the Defence Force. She had turned her back on the security she'd previously felt. Emma grinned, she didn't need it anymore. She was no longer a coward, hiding who she was.

***

Emma was jolted to consciousness by movement, by her arms being lifted, and a metallic scrape. *Oh no.* In the pre-dawn light a figure knelt above her. Dav—no, not David.

"I've been looking forward to this for some time." Patersall wiped his hands on his uniform, a sick grin on his face.

Emma tried to hit him but couldn't move her arms. She'd been handcuffed. "David!" she screamed.

A groan answered. David lay by the abandoned boat, bleeding from a gash in his head, his arms and legs tied together.

"He's not going to save you," Patersall scoffed.

Emma swallowed, trying to fight against the rising panic. "What are you doing here?"

"I was stuck guarding the boats. When I heard the gunshot, when I heard the speedboat, I knew the city faggots had got too smart for their own good, so I followed." He smiled. "Imagine my surprise when I saw you had stolen the boat." Kneeling above her, holding her handcuffed wrists above her head, he tore open her shirt, revealing her pale body to the frigid dawn.

"Get off me," she growled, trying to free her hands. No matter what happened, she was going to fight back with everything she had.

Patersall's laugh echoed through the trees. His hand touched her exposed skin and she flinched in disgust. As his hands travelled down her body, she looked around for a rock, for anything. But it was hopeless. There was a log, just out of reach, too heavy to lift.

"You aren't going to try anything stupid now, are you?"

Emma gritted her teeth and shook her head, her mind racing, looking for a way out. She was not going to let this bastard beat her.

"Didn't think so."

Emma clamped her legs shut, determined to make this as hard for him as possible. Anger surged through her, hating him for what he'd done to David, for what he'd already tried to do to her. He smiled as she fought back, and a nauseous dread built up inside her. The prick was loving this, watching her struggle and squirm. As she cried out for David, Patersall climbed on top of her and stared into her eyes with lust and victory.

He had her where he wanted. She fought the nausea and disgust that penetrated her soul as he reached down. *This is it.*

David shouted, and Patersall turned his attention to him for a moment. A moment was all she needed.

Emma pulled her legs back, aimed, and kicked her heel up into his face. The contact threw his head backwards. She lashed out with her foot again. After staggering to his feet, Patersall rubbed his jaw, glaring at her. Emma lay in the dirt, heart racing, her arms cuffed together. She struggled to her knees, then froze as Patersall drew a knife from a sheath on his belt.

He took a step forward, concentrating on his paralysed prey.

As he took another step, David kicked out at Patersall's legs, throwing him off balance. Patersall fell to his knees, slashing out with the knife.

David screamed.

Adrenaline surging through her body, Emma got to her feet. *I'm ready for you.* Blue eyes flashing, Patersall stood up, stepped forward and swung with his right fist. Ducking under the blow, his arm glanced off the top of her head as she stepped past him. She threw her elbow into his back. With a grunt, Patersall toppled forward. Emma spun, kicked him in the small of his back and sent him sprawling into the dirt, the knife falling from his hands.

She wasn't done.

Emma jumped on top of Patersall as he crawled forward to where the knife lay, dark with David's blood. Looping the chain of the handcuffs around his neck, she pulled her arms back, choking him.

Patersall bucked, threw his elbows back, trying to knock her off, but she refused to be moved. *I've got you, you bastard!* Breathing in harsh, ragged gasps, Patersall spat blood. Snarling, he jerked his head backwards and smashed it into Emma's face with a sickening crack.

With pain bursting through her skull, she almost slipped, almost let go. *I won't let you beat me.* Grunting and full of hatred, blood streaming down her face, Emma pulled back harder and harder on the chains, watching his face turn red, then purple, his bloodshot eyes bulging. Finally, he collapsed, unconscious, her weight driving him into the dirt.

Emma rolled off him, exhausted. But she couldn't stop. Fighting the pain, she wiped the blood off her face, picked up Patersall's knife, and staggered to where David lay.

When he'd been untied, David embraced her, giving her his strength, his warmth. "My arm." He groaned. "That shithead cut my arm." A dark stain spread under the right sleeve of his shirt, the thick cotton cut open, red with blood.

As Emma tried to calm her breathing, David searched Patersall's pockets for the handcuff keys. After being freed, she sat by the wooden boat, exhausted, her body shaking with fear, disgust and anger. *That bastard,* she thought as she buttoned her shirt with weak, trembling fingers and wrapped her arms around herself.

David cuffed Patersall with his own handcuffs and tied his legs together before sitting down next to Emma. His shirt sleeve was dark and dripping with blood. "I'm running out of goddamn limbs," he muttered.

Emma watched as David unbuttoned his shirt, taking it off to reveal the ragged cut across his upper arm. It was deep, overflowing with blood, but not dangerous. Not unless infection took hold. He grimaced as he dabbed antiseptic from the medkit over the wound and wrapped a clean bandage around it. She wanted to help, but she couldn't. She felt so defiled, so shaken and so sick it was all she could do to hold herself together.

Her eyes drifted between the sea and Private Patersall as David passed her a bottle of water.

"Drink. We need to get our fluids back."

She nodded. *And you need to see a doctor.*

"What do you want to do with that arsehole?" David asked. "Should we just leave him here?"

An idea struck her. "We need to get him out of that uniform."

Patersall groaned in pain as he returned to consciousness.

"Did you hear that, Private?" Emma growled as David stripped Patersall of his uniform. "I'm letting you live. We both know I've beat you twice now, you pathetic piece of shit. If you want to try me again, I'll be ready. I'll beat you again."

His cruel blue eyes looked up at her. A dangerous smile crossed his face.

"I almost hope you come after me again," she hissed. "Beating the crap out of you was kinda fun."

***

As the sun rose above the hill, David and Emma prepared to leave. They handcuffed Patersall into his boat, a rag in his mouth. He watched as David removed the oars, took his supplies and weapons, and cut the fuel lines. They pushed his boat out into the water, into the receding tide. If it took the boat, Patersall would be at the mercy of the seas.

Emma looked forward, to the mountain north of them, the end of Messinger's territory. To the future, to a world with hope.

David sighed as he watched the sun's rays bounce off the distant towers, the familiar silver, gold and blue of his submerged city.

Emma hoped Elise had listened to her tactics, that they would keep resisting the wrath of Messinger's army. "You were right, you know," Emma said, picking up the backpack and Patersall's F88. "The monsters are on the land, not in the sea. And I should know. I used to be one."

David smiled. "And now?"

"Now, I'm me. For the first time, I'm not hiding behind a uniform. I'm not hiding from myself."

CHAPTER TWENTY-FIVE

With a machine gun slung around his shoulder and a tree branch for a crutch, David followed Emma. They trekked into the bush, leaving the crashing of the waves and the cry of the gulls behind. *How the hell am I going to find Sal?* "Emma," he called, breaking the silence. "Where are we going?"

"You're not going to want to know."

"What are you talking about?"

"You've been shot. You need medical attention."

She can't mean . . . "We better not be going to a militia hospital."

"Trust me. I've got a plan."

The realisation hit him like a blow to the guts. *Patersall's uniform.* "I don't like the sound of this."

"I told you." She looked back at him with a smile behind her grey eyes. "But I know someone, a paramedic at the Ferntree Gully base. The uniforms should get us close enough to see her."

"Won't they be looking for us? Looking for you?"

"Only Jo knows what I look like. And besides, we both look a hell of a lot worse than we did two days ago."

David nodded, too exhausted to argue.

***

There was a clearing ahead. A smell he recognised. *Oh no.* His guts squirmed in disgust as they approached a road. Cars had been thrown through trees, flipped upside down, and—along with their occupants—had been left to rot. The smell was bad, but not as bad as the sight of the decaying bodies. Emma retched and David fought down the sickness, the bile, rising in his guts.

Emma pushed on north, picking her way uphill through the trees and bushes under the warm sun. David followed, grunting in pain with every step, his skin slick with sweat. A great pit, a grey-brown hole appeared, half-full of dark green water. They stopped, gasping in the fresh air, taking in the view. Below them to the west were flooded suburbs; residential houses and shops all under the sea. Wreckage and ruin, hopelessness and despair. To the north were suburbs bordering on farmland, acres and acres of cleared land. Beyond that, green tree-covered mountains. The Dandenong Ranges.

David asked the unspoken question. "How are we going to find Sal?"

Emma shook her head. "I don't know. I really don't." She looked up at him, anguish in her eyes. "I'm sorry. I don't know what I was thinking, telling him to come out east."

"I'm just glad you let him get away. He's too smart to let himself get caught twice."

"I hope you're right."

Me too. Out of nowhere, a sinking feeling solidified in the pit of David's gut. Sal was a fighter. He hated the militia. *Shit.* He couldn't just run from them.

Emma must have noticed his trembling hands. "What's wrong?"

"I think I know where Sal might be."

"Where?"

"You don't want to know."

***

His heart heavy, he followed Emma north, skirting around a few intact houses. It had been hours since they had started out, and they still had not seen a soul.

"Where is everybody?"

Emma said nothing, but adjusted her grip on the machine gun.

In the distance, a dog barked. People were out there, and David knew he and Emma were being watched. They pushed on, heading further north.

"I hope you know where you're going."

"Don't worry about that. I know where we are."

They crested a hill and took a breather under a tree. There was a football oval below and homes close together amongst the trees.

"We're almost there." Emma smiled.

"Wait—what's that?" David asked, pointing at the oval. There was a dark patch in the centre, and movement. Dread filled him as a figure dragged something into the middle of the field. Something heavy.

"That's what happens to people we don't like out these parts." A voice, deep and ominous. Right behind them.

David turned, facing the figure. Broad shouldered, shotgun in his hands, a menacing smile on his weatherbeaten face.

"We don't mean to trespass," Emma said. "We're just trying to get to the hospital."

"Well you're here now, whatever you meant to do."

"We won't be in your hair for long," David said. "Look mate, I've been shot, I've been stabbed. We aren't here looking to start trouble."

"You'll find trouble if your girl don't take her hand off that weapon."

"That ain't gonna happen," Emma growled. "I've got precious few rounds left, and I plan to use them on the militia. If you insist on getting in our way, I'm going to have to make an exception. We need to get to that fucking hospital."

"A cute thing like you against the militia? I'd like to see that."

"Believe it," David said. "They were the shitheads who shot me."

He looked them up and down. "If you want to use those guns against the ADF, I don't reckon I'll stop you. Those fuckers took my brother. Someone needs to fight back."

David nodded, then staggered towards the houses. "Let's get outta here," he said to Emma. Then, in a whisper, "and show me how to use these machine guns."

CHAPTER TWENTY-SIX

Her stomach full of anxiety, Emma led David through the trees and past buildings, edging closer to the Ferntree Gully hospital. The pale grey three-story building stood out above the nearby residential houses.

They reached an abandoned house, hidden from the street by thick bushes.

"You stay here with the guns, get into that uniform. I'm going to take a closer look."

David grimaced. "Be quick."

"I don't want to put my goddamn uniform on again either, believe me. But if we're going to get you fixed up, we need to."

Alone and defenceless, wearing Kintha's clothes, Emma approached the base. A barbed wire fence surrounded the hospital and the car parks, and the football oval nearby was covered with tents. Soldiers were everywhere. *Where was Jo?* Emma walked around the fence until she reached the entrance. A gate guarded by four soldiers, bunkered down behind a sandbag wall. Eyes dead ahead, she walked past and followed the barbed wire fence for another hundred metres. That's where she saw it. The emergency bay. Her heart rate quickened. An ambulance.

She turned back the way she had come. *How were they going to get in?* As she got close to the entrance an engine revved. She paused, heart racing, and turned to look at the ambulance. Its lights were on, and with a low roar, it began moving towards the gate.

Emma quickened her pace and reached the gate just before the ambulance. She turned, trying to look through the dark tinted windows. *Was Jo in there?* Her heart sank as the ambulance cruised through the gate, not slowing down. *She didn't see me. It wasn't her.* As the ambulance turned down the road, gaining speed, Emma broke into a run, tried to chase it down. She needed to know. Pushing through her pain, her exhaustion, she forced her battered body into a sprint.

It was no use, the ambulance didn't slow, didn't stop. But she couldn't give up. Emma forced her aching legs to keep going and followed the ambulance around a corner, pushing herself beyond her limits, her ragged heart bursting.

A figure darted into the middle of the road, right in front of the ambulance—a soldier, waving an assault weapon.

The ambulance screeched to a stop, the red of the brake lights blurring in Emma's vision. *What was happening?* She pushed herself on, a slow, aching jog, and watched as the limping soldier approached the ambulance, gun aimed at the driver.

The door opened. The driver stepped out, arms in the air. Red hair spilling out underneath a hat. It was her! It was Josephine!

"Josephine!" she cried, her choked voice tearing her aching throat.

The soldier—David—lowered his weapon and stepped back.

"Jo!" Emma cried again.

The driver turned, recognition lighting up her face.

Emma's heart lifted as she staggered forwards into her friend's embrace.

"What's happened—I heard you were MIA? I thought I'd never see you again!"

Emma could only squeeze her friend even tighter.

"We need to get out of here." David's voice was tense. "Somewhere safe."

"And who the fuck's that guy?"

***

Emma couldn't stop smiling as she climbed into the passenger seat and David got in the back.

Josephine, still shaken, drove them through the backstreets of Ferntree Gully. "I'm so glad to see you again. But you look like crap."

Emma tried to laugh, tears streaming down her cheeks.

Jo looked at her friend, concern clear behind her green eyes, and parked the van out of sight. "What is going on, Emma?"

A moment of fear. *What would Jo think?* She took a breath, steadied herself. "First, David's been shot in the leg. His arm's been cut up pretty bad."

Jo nodded and grabbed a medkit. "I'll patch him up best I can while you tell me the rest."

Anxiety churned in Emma's stomach as her

friend climbed out of the cabin. She took a moment before jumping out and following Jo to the rear of the ambulance.

"When where you shot?" Jo asked, rolling up the leg of David's jeans, her hands in sterile blue gloves. Blood leaked through the bandage.

"About six hours ago."

"Shit. You're doing well."

David grimaced as Jo prodded the wound.

Emma watched as her friend worked. "Jo, David's from the towers in the city. I was captured by them during the mission."

Josephine nodded. "I guessed that much."

"We'd taken his son the night before. We were ordered to capture anyone we could find, and Patersall and Basada found Salim." She sighed, and looked at David, her heart going out to him. "They beat him up, knocked him unconscious, dragged him to the boat. When we returned to the mainland, he bolted. I let him get away. I told him to go east."

Jo looked up at her, a question in her eyes.

"He was just a kid. I couldn't do it."

"So now you've joined them. Is that it?" she asked, turning back to David's leg.

"They're my people." Emma said, too scared to

look at her friend.

"What do you mean?"

Emma felt her friend's eyes on her. She looked up, met Jo's concerned gaze, then looked away.

"What is it, Emma? Are you okay?"

Hey chest tight with anxiety, Emma took a breath. *I need to do this.* "I'm like those people we arrest. That I *used* to arrest. That Messinger blames for the asteroid."

"Shit, you're gay?"

"I like women." Emma said, hesitant. "And men too. I'm bi." *Was her friend going to betray her? Turn her in?*

"Shit." Jo repeated. "All this time and you never said?"

Emma shook her head. "I was trying to hide it from myself for so long." Her voice shook, tears welled behind her eyes. "I pushed it down so far. But after Patersall attacked me, after the massacre, I couldn't hide from it, I couldn't run anymore." Emma's vision blurred, she stood there shaking, alone and exposed. She felt arms around her, her friend's embrace.

"It's okay, Emma. You're safe. I'll keep you safe."

CHAPTER TWENTY-SEVEN

"There you go, David. I've treated your wounds as best I can. If I tell you to stay off your feet for the next few weeks to let your leg heal, will you listen?"

David shook his head. "But thanks. And sorry for pulling that gun on you. Emma said she came here looking for a paramedic, so when I saw the ambulance . . ."

"So now what?" Josephine asked, looking between him and Emma. "I'm meant to be picking up patients from Box Hill and transporting them to Ferntree Gully. They'll expect me at Box Hill pretty soon."

"Help us," Emma pleaded. "The ADF,

Messinger, they've got to be stopped."

Jo shook her head. "I don't know. Messinger is an arsehole, and most of the brass have shit for brains. But what can we do? We're just three people. If they catch us . . . I mean, I just drive an ambulance. I'm no hero. I'm no rebel."

"Let's put the big questions aside," David said. "Can you help me find my son?"

"How in God's name do you expect to find him?"

"Sal's a fighter. He hates the militia."

"And?"

"I don't think he could see the militia harass or beat anyone and not try to intervene. My gut is telling me he's in a labour camp."

"Shit."

"All you need to do is drive us to where they're working."

Jo nodded. "I can do that."

***

David sat in the passenger seat as they drove through the suburbs. The afternoon sun shone on the ruined houses and frightened survivors as the ambulance sped past, negotiating rubble and ruined cars.

They slowed as they approached a labour camp. Scrawny figures cleared rubble off the road under the scrutiny of soldiers. They were being forced to carry bricks and slabs of concrete, dumping them into the waiting wheelbarrows. No Salim.

"How many labour crews are there?"

"Three."

They drove past another labour crew where a security guard punched a prisoner in the stomach. Again, no Salim.

"How can you let them keep doing this?" he asked, anger burning through him.

Jo shook her head and they drove away.

***

David was losing hope they'd find Sal. Maybe he was wrong that he'd been captured. That he couldn't resist fighting back against the militia. They drove down Whitehorse Road towards Box Hill, the multi-lane road littered with wrecks of cars, the ruins of two-story houses on either side.

Jo stopped the ambulance. The road ahead was blocked by smashed cars. Groups of handcuffed prisoners—under the supervision of three guards—were trying to tip the cars back onto their wheels and clear the road.

David stared at the scene, watching for any sign of his son. He was far too young, too weak to do this kind of work. *He should still be in school, dammit.*

There—a dark green jumper on the ground. A guard stood above him, kicking him. "That's him—that's Sal on the ground!"

"Shit. What are you going to do?"

"I'm going to get my son." He banged the glass panel separating the front and rear of the ambulance, letting Emma know it was time. Machine gun in hand, he jumped out of the cabin. His heart racing, he walked around the ambulance and opened the back door. "He's here."

Emma, dressed in her uniform, reached for her weapon. "How are we going to do this?"

"Ask nicely. Only shoot if we need to."

Adrenaline pumped through David's veins as he stepped out from behind the ambulance, Emma a footstep behind.

"What do you want?" A clean-shaven guard stepped forward. "We've got no need for an ambulance."

Not yet, you don't. "We're here for a prisoner."

"Can't help you. None of these lazy mongrels are going anywhere, are they, Coulter?" he asked, turning to the guard standing above Sal.

"Nope. Not 'til this section of road is clear and clean enough to eat off, Underhill."

David looked past the guard to where Sal lay, sprawled in the dirt at the feet of the second guard. He swallowed his fear and nausea, checked his grip on his machine gun.

The third guard sat on the hood of a car. All eyes were on Emma and David.

"With all due respect," Emma growled, "we're just following our orders. It can't be that hard to find another volunteer to take their place."

One prisoner edged away while the guards were distracted. As he turned and bolted, the guard sitting on the car shot him in the back.

"Stop!" David shouted.

"Looks like we needed that ambulance after all." The guard grinned as he slid his pistol onto his holster.

David and Underhill raised their weapons at the same time. "I asked you nicely," David growled, looking down the barrel of Underhill's pistol. "I'm done being nice. This is your last chance. Release the prisoners."

"You want them all now?" Coulter looked up, a

smile on his face. "They ain't all going to fit in your ambulance now, are they?"

"Why the hell to you even want these useless dipshits anyway?" asked Underhill. Behind him, the prisoners were moving, ducking behind cars. But not Sal. His green jumper lay motionless in the dirt. David's heart sank—maybe they were already too late.

"I won't ask again." David's finger was on the trigger, sweat pouring down his back. He took a step closer, trying to get a look at his son, his legs shaking.

"Stay where you are and drop your weapon." Underhill's voice was firm, threatening.

Behind him came a sharp cry. A prisoner wrapped his handcuffs around the neck of the guard who was perched on the car.

Coulter turned and fired. The prisoner's head was knocked backwards, blood spraying out behind him. Falling backwards, he dragged the guard off the car.

Emma burst past David, charging at Coulter. Underhill swung his pistol from David to Emma and fired.

Anger pumping through his veins, David raised the machine gun and squeezed the trigger. The weapon kicked back with every deafening round it fired.

Emma launched her body into Coulter's back and

sent him sprawling into the dirt. She drove her knee into his back and grabbed his arms, pulling them behind him.

As Underhill slumped to the ground in front of David—the front of his uniform already a dark crimson—the muffled sounds of struggle came from behind the car, then a single gunshot.

David left Underhill in the dirt, eyes only for Sal.

Emma was still struggling with Coulter, the arm of her uniform covered in blood.

Stepping past them, dread filling him, David knelt by his son. "Sal, it's me. Wake up." Hopelessness and despair filled him. He was too late.

Salim lay on his back, his right eye swollen and bruised, his jumper stained with blood and dirt, his lips dry and cracked.

"Come on, son. I've come for you," David pleaded. *Like I promised.* His eyes full of hot tears, he checked Salim's neck for a pulse. Faint, but there.

"I'm going to get you outta here," David said, reaching his hands under Salim's back and legs. He lifted him up and stumbled forward, shocked at how little he weighed.

Sal groaned in his arms, his left eye opening.

"It's me, Sal. I've got you." A wave of relief washed over David. "I'm going to get you out of here."

"Shit Da, what are you doing in that uniform?" Sal's voice was weak and ragged.

Tears streamed down David's cheeks. Sal was alive. "That's a good bloody question." He'd been given another chance. He wouldn't screw up again.

CHAPTER TWENTY-EIGHT

Emma wrestled with the guard on the ground, pain shooting through her shoulder. Her left arm was weak, she couldn't use it. She couldn't grab both his arms.

Footsteps approached in time with her racing heart.

"I'm coming!"

Emma smiled as Josephine knelt next to her and grabbed the guard's other arm. Together they handcuffed him, ignoring his cries of protest.

"You've got to let me look at that arm," said Jo.

She glanced down. Blood stained the sleeve of her uniform.

"How does it feel?"

Emma gritted her teeth as Jo explored her wound. Looking away, she saw David approaching, carrying Sal in his arms. Her heart lifted as she saw the kid open his eyes and look at her. "Hey Sal, good to see you again." She blinked back tears.

"You." His eyes widened after a moment. "You're the one who let me go."

She nodded.

"Are you okay, Emma?" David asked.

"Yeah. It hurts like a bastard, and my shoulder's probably fucked, but I think so. How about Sal?"

"I feel like I've been hit by a truck," said Salim, his voice weak.

"We need to get you both back to the ambulance," said Jo.

Several prisoners stood nearby, one holding the guard's pistol. He stepped forward, unsure and afraid.

"You guys aren't real soldiers, are you?" he asked, tension in his voice.

"I'm not," David said. "I'm just here for my son."

"I was," said Emma, guilt surging through her. "And I did some fucked-up things. But I'm trying to make amends. You're free to go. Don't let them catch you again."

"You were awesome, the way you ran at that guard. The way you stood up to those wankers," the prisoner said, a grin on his face. "If you're going to do shit like that again, I want in. We want to help, to fight back."

"All right, everyone back," snapped Jo. "She's been shot and I need to make sure the kid's okay. Give us a minute so I can fix her up and stop the bleeding."

Dragged to her feet, Emma followed Jo to the ambulance.

"We'll leave the guard in your care," David said to the freed prisoners before following, bringing Sal with him.

****

Inside the ambulance, Jo took Sal's temperature and blood pressure, ran her hands over his body checking for injuries. Satisfied, she turned to Emma and cut away the blood-soaked uniform around her wound.

Emma looked away from the aching hole in her shoulder, from the blood dripping down her arm.

"I'm going to start by giving you a local anaesthetic." Josephine said.

Emma nodded and closed her eyes as Jo

approached, needle in hand. The needle pierced her torn flesh, piling agony onto agony, and Emma squeezed her eyes shut, trying to block out the pain. When she opened her eyes, Josephine was cutting into her shoulder with a scalpel. Emma fought against the pain and the nausea churning in her stomach. Blood was everywhere. Her blood. *I need to stay awake.*

David and Sal watched, their faces pale.

"So David, are you and Sal going to go back home now?" she asked, forcing the words out.

David looked at Sal, then back to her. "Would you come with us?"

Emma shook her head. "I want to. I know I'd be accepted, it's just . . ."

"What?"

Emma focused on her friend as her consciousness began to slip. "Jo knows. Where we go."

"Knows what?" Sal asked.

Josephine's brow was creased in concentration as she worked, then smiled to herself. "What Emma's saying is that we go where we're needed." She looked at Emma, her eyes full of warmth and understanding.

Emma nodded. "I'm still needed here," she whispered, her voice weak. "We're still needed." *To take down Messinger. To stand up against all his bullshit.*

"I understand." David reached out and squeezed Emma's hand. "If you plan on taking on Messinger, don't think I'm going to let you do it alone."

"And I'm with you," Jo said. "There has to be a better way than hatred and fear."

Emma nodded, her heart bursting. *There is. It's love. And it's hope.*

ABOUT THE AUTHOR

Austin P. Sheehan is a writer of speculative fiction, a lover of language, literature and '90s TV. Armed with a psychology degree, he went out into the world to further study humanity, and now prefers the company of his wife and rescue greyhounds.

Austin grew up in Victoria's high country, and despite living in Melbourne for ten years, still feels at home amongst the mountains. In fact, you'll often find mountains in his stories, whether they are science fiction, fantasy, alternative history or horror. If you want to discover what secrets are hidden in the mountains, go to www.austinpsheehan.com or find him on twitter @AustinPSheehan.

Austin's novella 'Submerged City' (part of the Drowned Earth series by Aussie Speculative Fiction) was published in 2019. His short stories have also been published in 'A Bond of Words' (Scout Media), 'Beginnings' (Aussie Speculative Fiction) and 'Flash Fiction Addiction' (Zombie Pirate Publishing). His microfiction appears in 'Curses & Cauldrons' (Blood Song Books) and the 'Worlds' 'Monsters' and 'Apocalypse' anthologies by Black Hare Press.

ABOUT DEADSET PRESS

Deadset Press is the publishing imprint for Aussie Speculative Fiction – a community aimed at supporting Australian and Kiwi authors. You can learn more at:

www.aussiespeculativefiction.com

ABOUT THE SERIES

Drowned Earth is a series of eight standalone novellas, set in a shared world.

Prequel: Shards of Silver by Alanah Andrews

Debbie is on board a ship when an asteroid collides with Antarctica, causing a tsunami. And it's heading her way…
(eBook Only: Free Download)

The Rise by Sue-Ellen Pashley

The great Rise means that resources are scarce and not readily shared. But with her best friend's life at stake, along with some stranded refugees, Katie James knows she must prove there's more to being human than just existing. Even if that puts her on the same kill list.

Fire Over Troubled Water by Nick Marone

Despite winds, torrential rains, storms, and bushfires, a fresh water merchant searches for his lost daughter among the autonomous island communities of flooded eastern New South Wales.

Submerged City by Austin P. Sheehan

Melbourne is under martial law, overseen by general Messinger—an extremist who believes the flood is God's retribution against the left-wing agenda...

Tides of War by Marcus Turner

After discovering a strange man in a row boat, Maria wages war on the lotus cities—clandestine floating communities off the coast of Victoria that are reserved for the wealthy.

The Jindabyne Secret by Jo Hart

With nothing but a map and a rickety solar truck, Jax journeys to the top secret fresh water facility at Lake Jindabyne—one of the few fresh water lakes left in Australia. What he discovers there could be the key to saving his whole community, as long as the government doesn't kill him first.

River of Diamonds by S. M. Isaac

Who would want to leave one of the last idyllic settlements since the Rise? Rosa has a map, a mercenary, and a hope to salvage a future for the world.

Salvaged by C.A. Clark

Cassie lives in the safe haven of academics on the anchored city of new Melbourne. After a diving incident she is rescued by a territorial beach combing gang who trade goods washed up by the frequent storms. Cassie wishes she had never taken her home for granted.

Emoto's Promise by Shel Calopa

Five hundred years after the flood, can Macie defeat the technology which has enslaved the last remaining humans in the walled city of Darwin?

ALSO BY DEADSET PRESS

Annual Anthologies

Beginnings: Australian Speculative Fiction Vol. 1

Journeys: Australian Speculative Fiction Vol. 2

Zodiac Series

Capricorn

Aquarius

Pisces

www.aussiespeculativefiction.com